CLAWFUL REFLECTIONS

A Wonder Cats Mystery Book 10

HARPER LIN

ISBN: 978-1-987859-68-3

www.harperlin.com

MRS. KITT

"**S**omeone's coming to the door," Treacle told me as he slinked along the windowsill, pushing the curtains aside. His ears perked up as his green eyes widened with curiosity.

"At this hour?" I cringed. "It's not even seven o'clock in the morning. I thought only lunatics like us who had to go to work were up at this hour."

Just then the doorbell rang, and there was a knock that followed.

"Who is it?" I whispered to my cat, who had taken a seat on the sill.

"*I don't know,*" Treacle replied.

"Should I answer it?" I asked nervously. It wasn't often that strangers came to my house. "Are they holding pamphlets or a clipboard?"

"No. It's just one older lady, and she's in pajamas. I think she's from next door."

I was dressed in jeans and a T-shirt, but my feet were bare, and my hair was still wet from the shower. I padded over to the door and looked through the peephole to see a rather distraught Mrs. Kitt.

"It is the neighbor," I whispered as I slipped the chain out of the slot and turned my dead bolt. I opened the door and put on my friendliest face. I'm afraid it came off more like a grimace. "Hi, Mrs. Kitt."

"Hello, honey. I'm so sorry to bother you." She held her hands nervously in front of her. Her early-morning ensemble was pink flannel pajama pants with gray smiling cats on them and a matching button-down top that was covered by a baggy hoodie with a zipper up the front. Mrs. Kitt wore her hair cut short and dyed a soft auburn color. This morning it was pressed on one side and poofy on the other.

"No, please. Is everything all right?" I hoped there wasn't some issue that required her to use my phone, fridge, or shower. My house was a disaster because I'd been working longer hours. Sometimes I didn't make it to the bedroom before I shed my clothes to flop down in front of the television. I also finished one, maybe two, pints of ice cream in the bathroom. The empty containers were there to prove it.

"Well, I'm watching the Lourdeses' cats while they are on vacation." She pointed toward her house. "They've gone to Europe for a second honeymoon. Can you believe that?" Mrs. Kitt clapped her hands together, hunching her shoulders and batting her eyes as if it were all so romantic.

"The Lourdeses?" I tilted my head to the right.

"They are on the other side of my house." She nodded.

"Oh, yes." I didn't know their last name was Lourdes. I always referred to them as the "babe couple." They were constantly within arm's reach of each other, pawing and kissing, and they called each other babe...loudly...while they did yard work or unloaded groceries or walked to the mailbox. Weird. They were sort of like my cousin Bea and her husband, Jake, if their public displays of affection were to be injected with steroids.

"Well, I thought I had enough cat food to get me to the end of the week, but it appears I've run out, and I have to go to work. Can you spare a can?" Mrs. Kitt acted as if she were requesting a kidney.

"My gosh, of course I can. Just a second."

"She's going to invite you to one of her snake-handling services. The cat food was just a way to get you to open the door." Treacle licked his paw.

"Very funny," I replied telepathically as I grabbed three cans of cat food. *"Don't make me give her your favorite salmon-flavored Fancy Feast."*

"You wouldn't dare!"

I held the cans close to me as I strolled back to the door. Treacle peeked from behind the curtain to see if I was indeed giving away his favorite flavor. I mouthed the word *chicken* to which he whipped his tail.

I'd had the ability to communicate telepathically with animals since as far back as I could remember. It was my gift. The only time I ever felt it was a curse was when I went to the zoo when I was a teenager. No one would believe how noisy and rude birds are. I'd have expected it in the monkey house. However, they surprised me by shouting encouragement to each other and the people who came to visit them. It was quite uplifting. Tony Robbins didn't encourage as well as monkeys. But the beautifully colored cockatoos and parrots flitting back and forth like elegant, vibrant pieces of tissue paper would put drunken sailors to shame. To say I was shocked would be an understatement. Needless to say, I didn't go to the zoo anymore.

"Here you go, Mrs. Kitt. Will three be enough?"

"Oh, thank you so much." Mrs. Kitt took the cans. "Yes. This is plenty. When I go to the store, I'll replace these for you."

"Don't worry about it." I waved my hand in front of me. "I've got plenty. It's not going to put me in the poorhouse."

"Well, thank you again, dear. Tell your aunt Astrid I said hello." She waved and hurried back to her property. I shut the door and looked at Treacle again.

"I think that is the longest conversation I've ever had with that woman." I shrugged as I went back to the bathroom to dry my hair and finish getting ready for work. "Usually I just wave and run in the house."

As I held my head upside down, with the hairdryer aimed at my hair, Treacle came into the bathroom.

"Did you know the babe couple had cats?" I shouted above the noise.

"*Yes. They stay inside.*" Treacle sniffed the air before flopping down on the floor. "*I think there are only two of them.*"

I shut off the dryer and flipped my hair up and

over my head before I tied it back in a ponytail. It was important to keep it out of my face at work. Especially since my family's coffee shop got such a nice write-up in the local paper.

The Wonder Falls Gazette said that the Brew-Ha-Ha Café put a spell on the neighborhood with its creative desserts and specialty hot teas. It was a rather appropriate choice of words since the Green-stones, my aunt Astrid, my cousin Bea, and myself, were indeed all witches. But no one in the town was aware. It was a secret we'd done pretty well keeping. Especially since the town of Wonder Falls had had more than its fair share of paranormal incidents. There were places that seemed to be beacons for this kind of activity. Some places you couldn't walk outside your house without catching a fuzzy glimpse of Bigfoot or looking out your window to see an unidentified flying object. Wonder Falls was like that. But that didn't make it any less our home.

"Are you ready? I think it is supposed to be a nice day outside," I said as I stroked Treacle's smooth black fur. His green eyes winked lazily as his purring motor started up.

"I smell rain."

"Are you kidding? It looked sunny to me." I scooped the cat into my arms and carried him to the front door. I grabbed my keys, opened the door, and stepped outside. Treacle wasted no time hopping down and giving my legs a good rubbing with his head. While I was locking up, I saw Mrs. Kitt hurrying to the house on the other side of hers with the cans in her hand. She'd changed into a long skirt and a boxy T-shirt. Her hair was still lopsided, but perhaps that was her signature look.

"I see Bea coming. Are you coming to the café with me, or are you going to conquer the neighborhood first?"

Treacle looked around, his nose twitching as he continued to sniff the air.

"I think I'll see what's happening. I'll meet you at the café later," he said as he quickly turned and trotted off, slinking between a couple of thick bushes and out of view.

As usual, I telepathically yelled for him to be careful and be home before dark so I wouldn't worry. My own thoughts sounded like my aunt Astrid when she said the same thing to Bea and me when we went out as teenagers.

I hurried across the street, where I waved to my cousin as she closed the door to her house and hurried across her porch. Before she made it down the front steps of her house, Jake yanked the door open and trotted out in his pajama bottoms and no shirt.

He slipped his arms around Bea, quickly giving her a kiss on the lips and a squeeze goodbye.

"She's just going to work down the street! She's not joining the Foreign Legion!" I shouted at them, smirking. It took me two seconds to regret my decision to yell. Jake charged at me, scooping me in his arms and swinging me around in a circle.

"Cath! I haven't seen you in so long!" He was practically screaming for all the neighborhood to hear.

"Would you put me down? Someone's going to call the cops on you. How will that look? Wonder Falls's chief detective taken into custody for displaying spastic behavior toward his cousin-in-law."

"Good morning, Cath. You are always such a ray of sunshine." Jake finally set me down. No matter how hard I tried, I couldn't hide my smile.

"You are the only one who can get her to smile before eight o'clock, Jake," Bea said as she caught up to us.

"That wasn't a smile. It was a scowl. You of all people should know the difference," I replied, shaking my head.

Jake gave Bea one more kiss before heading back to the house and slamming the front door shut.

"Hey, do you know the Lourdeses?" I asked as we headed in the direction of the café.

"Turk and Renee?" she asked.

"His name is Turk? Turk Lourdes?" There was no hiding my snarkiness. "Why am I shocked yet not shocked?"

"I know them enough to wave and say hi," Bea said. "They are an adorable couple."

"Couple of what?" I asked.

"Very funny. Why do you ask?" Bea swung her purse over her shoulder. She was the complete opposite of me, wearing a pretty skirt that came to her ankles and a sweater with big yellow flowers on it.

"Oh, Mrs. Kitt is watching their cats and ran out of cat food this morning. She asked to borrow a couple cans until she can get to the store. I just didn't know the real names of those people." I cleared my throat.

"What did you think their name was?"

I explained my nickname to Bea, who chuckled and shook her head.

"Cath, I really don't know how Tom puts up with you. He's such a romantic, and you are such a..."

"Careful, cousin. I'm an expert at sarcasm, and

I'm not afraid to use it." I put up my fists like I was going to fight.

"I was going to say skeptic. You need to open your heart a little more." Bea gently nudged me with her elbow. "You guys have been dating for a while. I'm not trying to butt into your business, but I thought things would have progressed a little further by now."

"You mean like wedding bells?" I looked at her curiously.

"I don't know, Cath. I can't say I'm not always hoping. You know, helping you pick out wedding colors and your dress and, of course, my maid-of-honor dress. Tom would certainly make a good husband."

Bea was a hopeless romantic. I knew her heart was in the right place, but it was hard for me to tell her that things with Tom weren't sailing so smoothly.

"I care about him. A lot. And I think he's so handsome and funny."

"So, what's holding you back?"

"If I knew, Bea, I'd have gotten rid of whatever it was a long time ago." I smiled, eager to change the subject. "That Mrs. Kitt is a character, isn't she?"

We walked the rest of the way to the café and saw

the lights inside were already on. Aunt Astrid was inside getting things in order.

"I think Mom would have a heart attack if you and I showed up earlier than her." Bea chuckled.

"We'd have to bring our sleeping bags and just spend the night. I swear she was probably already here half an hour after we closed last night," I replied. "I wonder what she knows about Mrs. Kitt. Mrs. Kitt told me, *'Say hi to your aunt for me.'* I didn't know she knew Aunt Astrid. Of course she's only lived next door to me for seven years."

"Yeah, hardly enough time to get to know some-one," Bea teased.

When we finally got to the café and Aunt Astrid let us in, I was surprised at what she had to say about Mrs. Kitt.

2

RUDIMENTARY

"Oh, yes. I really should give her a call," Aunt Astrid said after I told her about my visitor. "She's a clairvoyant."

"Really?" I nearly choked on my coffee as I started to chuckle. "I'd never have pegged her as clairvoyant. I guess I expect everyone with a 'gift' to look as good as us." I wrinkled my face and crossed my eyes.

It was Aunt Astrid's turn to laugh as she flipped her long silver hair. She had a boho style that made her look like a modern-day gypsy. That wasn't far from the truth since she regularly did psychic readings for the folks in town. But her real gift was her ability to see multiple dimensions at once. People often thought she was staring into space or maybe daydreaming when, in reality, she was seeing what we couldn't. Things on different planes shifted and moved without us ever noticing. But she saw it all. Her gift also caused her to walk slowly and maneuver herself around as if she'd had a couple drinks.

"She's a sweet older lady," Bea said in Mrs. Kitt's defense.

"I didn't say she wasn't," I protested.

"She's just a trendsetter. Someone who marches to the beat of their own drum," Bea continued.

"Hey, I like her," I continued. "She's a neighbor who, in seven years, has only bothered me once. Today. That's a wonderful person if ever I knew one. Plus, it's usually the empaths who are the cockeyed, wobbly weirdos. She's just a plain old clairvoyant."

It only took a second for Bea to turn around and stick her tongue out at me. Of course, she was an empath. Her amazing ability to absorb people's pain and heal them was something so great she had to eventually tell Jake that she came from a family of witches and had this gift. If he was nervous about it, or us, he never showed it.

"Actually, Cath is right," Aunt Astrid interrupted

as she took her seat at her usual table for two at the end of the counter where she worked on the financial books while Bea and I got the café ready to open.

"That I'm a cockeyed, wobbly weirdo? Thanks, Mom." Bea huffed.

"In addition to that," Aunt Astrid said, "Mrs. Kitt's abilities are rudimentary at best. Every once in a while, she can help someone find their keys or locate a lost dog. But that is the extent of it. She told me she has no desire to hone her skill."

"Well, you can't blame her for that," I said. "It's a lot of responsibility. And she's obviously not that organized if she forgot to buy cat food for the neighbors' cats she's babysitting. Have you ever talked to the Lourdeses?"

My aunt mentioned seeing them once or twice, but she never had a reason to speak to them.

"Cath thinks they are too affectionate," Bea teased as she filled the giant silver coffee pot with water.

"Hey, there is a time and place for kissy-face, and it isn't in the middle of the driveway with all the world gawking at you. Plus, a guy named Turk ought to be out there washing his car or cutting the grass. You know, doing manly things. Not chasing after his wife, carrying grocery bags. 'Hold the door for me, babe.' 'Oh, I sure will, babe.' It's creepy." I rolled my eyes.

"Of all the things you've seen in life, that is what creeps you out?" Bea asked.

"Yes. Yes, it is," I replied as I stuffed more napkins into the dispensers.

"What does Tom think of that?" Aunt Astrid asked.

I felt my cheeks heat up, and I shook my head as I avoided looking at Bea or my aunt.

"I was just asking her that on the way over here," Bea said.

"Tom and I are in a place where we are just sort of taking in the view. We don't know what direction to go in, and so we are just standing still for a bit. You know, to catch our breath, get our bearings."

The truth was I had no idea what Tom thought about a lot of things. It wasn't that I didn't care. But from where I was sitting, there seemed to be too many things in our way.

I guess I thought that when it was right, the path would be a little clearer. There wouldn't be so many obstacles in the way.

The main one being his mother.

Patience Warner.

She hated me.

And no matter how many times Tom said that her opinion didn't matter, that she would learn to love me, to get to know me, I didn't just doubt it. I downright didn't believe it at all. It made me sad, but at the same time, I couldn't help feeling a little relieved. There was an excuse for me to not get too attached.

It was selfish. That knot kept turning in my gut whenever Tom tried to break through my boundaries. He was becoming frustrated and short with me on occasion, but I just couldn't stop myself.

I'm sure if I sat in a psychiatrist's chair, he'd tell me that I was holding back because, when I was nine years old, my mother was taken from me. I loved her. She was all I knew of the world, and in order to save me, she sacrificed herself. Yes, I still felt guilty. Yes, I was afraid if I loved anyone like that, they'd be taken from me too. Yes, I thought it was my fault. Had I not been in that bedroom, had I not had this "gift" of speaking to animals, maybe those two grotesque arms wouldn't have come from beneath my bed. Maybe they wouldn't have grabbed hold of my mother as she got me safely out of the way. Maybe she wouldn't have been dragged underneath the bed. That was my fault, no matter how many people tried to tell me it wasn't. And if it happened to her, it could happen to anybody. Including Tom.

Yes, it was selfish. But I didn't want to feel responsible for him getting hurt. And if I let him get any closer, that would be exactly what would happen. Something in my gut told me so. And I'd learned to listen to that gut feeling. Blake Samberg, Jake's partner on the force, told me more than once to always trust my gut.

"It sounds to me like you are stalling," Aunt Astrid said.

"Stalling? The engine never got started," I joked.

"Hey, is that Blake?" Bea asked, pointing across the street. I hated to admit it, but my heart jumped in my chest, and I tried not to look so interested as I stretched my neck and squinted my eyes.

"That looks like him and Jake," I said. "They don't look too good."

Something had happened that had them running toward the café. We weren't even officially open for the day. They knew this. For them to be coming over now had to mean something was wrong.

Quickly, Bea scooted around the counter and hurried to the door, unlocking it and pulling it open. The happy little jingle bells made their music as they clanged against the glass.

"What's wrong?" she asked as they stepped in. It was Blake who came up to me. The look of worry in his eyes scared me. He was the first to speak.

"Cath, we just heard over the radio. Tom has been shot."

3

DEVIL WORSHIPPER

For a second, everything stopped. The clock. The coffee percolating. My heart.

"What?" I muttered. My voice didn't even sound like my own. It was like someone else was doing the talking while I just moved my mouth.

"He responded to an 043. Domestic assault," Jake said as I looked up at Blake. "From what his partner called in, they showed up at the residence. The woman was high, drunk, maybe both. She and her boyfriend were arguing."

I just stood there, staring. What was I supposed to do? How was I supposed to react? I couldn't think. Not a single thought came into my head. I just looked at Bea, who was holding Jake's hand as he spoke. Aunt Astrid had her hand to her mouth. I didn't even feel Blake's hands holding mine until I squeezed them.

"Just as they knocked on the door, the woman ran and retrieved a gun from another room. She opened fire at the door, her boyfriend, anything." Jake looked at Bea.

"They're rushing him to St. Joseph Hospital," Blake said quietly. "Come on. I'll drive you there."

I nodded, swallowing hard as Blake led me to the car, leaving Bea, Jake, and Aunt Astrid at the café. He opened the door for me. I got in like we were just heading off to the grocery store.

I didn't speak while he drove. He had the portable red light slapped on the top of the car and a siren coming from somewhere. The cars parted for us like we were royalty. Except I couldn't enjoy it. Normally, I'd be thrilled to ride shotgun in a cop car with the siren going and light flashing. But I felt embarrassed. I didn't want anyone to see me or see Blake making such a fuss.

"Is he dead?" I asked.

"I don't know, Cath." Blake gripped the steering wheel nervously. He would have told me if Tom were already gone. Blake was one of those guys who knew how to rip a Band-Aid off. Quick and fast and then it's all over with but the remaining sting.

It felt like we were moving in slow motion. I was sure everyone we passed was staring and knew it was me in Blake's car. The people walking down the street, they had their loved ones waiting for them. They had their boyfriends and husbands safe at work or home. They weren't worried about them at all. Was I the only one?

Finally, we pulled up into the emergency parking. Blake pulled the car into a slot, leaving the light on top, hopped out, and quickly ran around to my side to open the door. I took his hand, and within minutes we were inside the building. With his badge in his hand, he asked at the information desk where Tom was. I saw a whole corral of wheelchairs and wanted to flop down in one and have him wheel me to Tom. My legs were getting weaker by the second. This was all becoming too real.

The person at the information desk pointed us to the emergency room, where there were dozens of stalls of people in various states of, well, emergency. I had expected to see Tom sitting at the end of a bed with maybe a bloody shirt where the bullet hit him in the shoulder or the arm. Maybe through his leg or something. He'd look up at me with those blue eyes, and they'd twinkle as he'd smile, shaking his head.

"Can you believe this?" he'd say, wincing.

But I didn't see him. There were a bunch of nurses hustling around. Now and then, a doctor came from somewhere only to disappear somewhere else.

"They said he was in 14G," Blake said. There were little signs above each stall with different letters and numbers. I couldn't read them. I'd forgotten my letters.

When we finally located 14G, it was empty. I let out a deep breath. Maybe he was released already. I looked to Blake, whose face had turned gray.

"What is it?" I asked. Obviously, he knew something and wasn't telling me.

"The 'G' numbers are for life-threatening emergencies," he said matter-of-factly. "If he isn't here, he's either in surgery or…"

"Or?" I whispered, feeling my eyes fill with tears. I bit my tongue to keep them back. This was all going to turn out fine. If I started blubbering all over myself, I was going to feel like an idiot when I finally saw Tom. This wasn't the movies.

"Sit down, Cath," Blake said, quickly pulling up a chair.

I hadn't realized that I was losing the feeling in my legs. I flopped down in the plastic chair in stall 14G while Blake took three long strides to reach the nurses' station in the center of the emergency admittance area.

A pretty blonde with purple scrubs typed a few things on her computer and said something to Blake that set him off. He pointed in my direction. He held up his badge. The nurse shrugged and said a few more things. Blake nodded and shook his head. When he came back to me, he put his hands in his pockets.

"Come on, Cath. Let's go wait in the waiting room."

"Can't we wait here? Won't they be bringing him back here?" I asked. The truth was I wasn't sure I could move. My whole body felt like it was encased in lead.

"He's had to go into surgery. The bullet went through his chest."

"But he was wearing a bulletproof vest, right?" Weren't they required to wear that? It was standard issue. At least that was what they said on all the cop television shows.

"Come on, Cath. I'll get you a cup of coffee." Blake helped me up and led me to the official waiting room. There were a couple other people there, but they looked relaxed, bored even.

"Why are we in here?" I asked.

"The nurse said that Tom is about to go into surgery," Blake said in that monotone he always used to state just the facts, ma'am. "The doctor will tell us what he can."

"When?"

"I'm not sure." He patted my back gently. "I'll get you a coffee. Just wait here."

Blake's reply wasn't comforting. Now that I was in this other room, I didn't feel like sitting down. I walked to the window and looked outside. It was such a pretty day. The sun was out. There were a few puffy white clouds against the blue backdrop. People were driving in and out of the parking lot. Not everyone who came here was in the shape Tom was in. Some people were having casts removed or giving birth or getting X-rays. For some reason, I felt like I was the only one here who was scared. Nothing made me feel more selfish, but it was the truth.

Then, as if I couldn't feel any worse, I heard my name being called.

"Cath. Cath Greenstone. What are you doing here?"

I turned around to see Tom's mother, Patience. She looked at me over her wire-rimmed glasses. She hadn't been crying. Her makeup was still impeccable. I, on the other hand, suddenly realized my eyes were stinging with tears that were in a nonstop wave down my cheeks.

"Detective Samberg brought me here when he heard over the radio that Tom had been shot," I muttered. "Did they tell you anything?"

"Did who tell me anything?" she snapped.

"The giant rabbit at the door. The doctor, for Pete's sake!" My voice cracked with frustration.

"You mean the doctor wouldn't share any information with you because you are *just* the girlfriend? I'm his mother. I'm family." She waved a finger in my face. "And I don't want you here."

"I have every right to be here, Patience." Tears ran down my cheeks. "I'm worried about him too. I just want to know if he's going to be okay and then..."

"And then what? You'll leave? Only to come back again. Really, Cath. You're like a bad penny," she scoffed. "You need to get out of here. I know what you are, and you aren't good for my son."

Just then, Blake came back with a coffee in his hand. He saw me crying and quickly pieced together what was going on with this Dolly Parton look-alike.

"Can I help you, ma'am?" He reached into his jacket pocket and pulled out his badge.

"Yes, you can remove this woman from the hospital. She's a danger to my son and, frankly, probably everyone else in here." Patience crossed her arms.

"She has a right to be here, Mrs....?"

"Patience Warner, Officer," Patience hissed. "That woman is the reason my son is in there."

"What?" I cried.

"If you weren't in the picture, he'd be able to concentrate. He wouldn't have gotten in this position. Instead of focusing on his work, he was distracted, wondering what your problem is and why you are the way you are."

"Mrs. Warner, you need to calm down." Blake stepped in between her and me.

"She's probably put a spell on him." She pointed madly at me. Blake was no obstacle for Patience Warner. "You know she's a devil worshipper, don't you? God only knows what kind of sinister, deviant things she's mixed up in."

"Patience. What are you saying?" I stammered.

"I want security!" she yelled. "Security! Get this witch, this devil worshipper out of here! She'll curse all of you!" Her voice was like a blow horn.

I looked around the waiting room. A crowd had started to gather, and they all looked at Patience and me like we were a disturbing sideshow attraction. It was a disgusting display, but they couldn't look away.

"Mrs. Warner. This is a hospital. People don't need you upsetting them further," Blake commanded. She looked up at him and sneered.

"You can see what she is, but you don't do anything," Patience continued. "Mark my words, everyone who is here right now, your loved ones won't get well. Not while she's here!"

I knew the truth about Patience. Aunt Astrid had seen it, and Bea too. She had her own supernatural gifts, but she didn't use them to help anyone. Obviously, from this display.

One of the men in the waiting room slipped out the door and brought back a rather large security guard.

"I don't know what's going on, but you ladies can't be making a scene in here." He was tall and muscular and had a Taser on his hip.

Blake tried to talk to him, but a badge didn't seem to mean too much when Patience made it clear we were not family.

"She's just the whore my son is dating," she spat to the security guard. "She has no relation to us."

The security guard looked at me sympathetically

but shook his head. I stood there with my mouth hanging open like I was trying to catch flies.

"You're out of line, Mrs. Warner!" Blake shouted, making her jump as her eyes widened. "There is no need for that kind of talk. Cath is just concerned. We all are."

Patience didn't say another thing but instead started to cry to the security guard about her son getting shot while on duty. It was an amazing act. But even though I couldn't see what was around her like Aunt Astrid could and I couldn't read her aura like Bea could, it didn't take any special gift to see Patience was disturbed.

The security guard started to get nervous when Patience didn't stop. I was beyond shocked and afraid if I started to speak, I'd say something that I'd regret. Thankfully, Blake was there and spoke over Patience to the security guard.

"We're leaving, Officer." He reached out his hand, and the security guard shook it, nodding and instructing us we could call and get an update on the patient's condition.

"No, you won't!" Patience continued. "I'll make sure they don't tell you anything! Not a single word!"

Blake took my hand and started to lead me out of the room.

"Patience, why?" I muttered as Blake pulled me past her.

"Because you're evil," she hissed.

Blake practically had to drag me out of the hospital. My legs had gone numb. As if the situation wasn't bad enough, Patience had to throw a one-two punch and put me down for the count.

I wanted my aunt. I wanted someone to take me in their arms and say it was all going to be okay, that there was something wrong with Patience, and that there was nothing wrong with me.

But there was something wrong with me. I was a witch. I was never going to be seen as normal or kind or helpful. But Patience was a witch too. Why wouldn't she want to work together to help her son?

Normally, I liked being alone. Solitude never frightened me. But right now, I felt lonely and isolated. I felt like no one could understand what those words Patience just uttered did to my heart.

Blake led me to his car, and before I could get in, he took me in his arms and held me tightly.

"It'll be okay, Cath." His cologne was subtle, but I always liked it. He smelled like sweet spices that were used to make a fall rum drink or something. I couldn't help but melt into him. I cried a little bit but tried to keep the hysterics to a minimum. "That woman is not well."

"I don't know, Blake," I sniffed. "Maybe she is right about me."

"No." His voice was soft. "You are the most genuine person I know. If she had any sense, she'd see that too. What you see is what you get with Cath Greenstone. And what you get is more than most people deserve."

Before I could stop myself, I wrapped my arms around Blake and hugged him tightly.

Again, the car ride back to the café was a quiet one. But it was easier to relax without the siren and the red light drawing attention to us. We were nothing more than another car on the road.

"What am I going to say to Aunt Astrid and Bea?" I muttered. "How do I tell them what that woman said? I'm humiliated. I didn't even get any information on Tom's condition. It was a big waste of time to go there."

"There is more than one way to get information, Cath. You have plenty of experience doing just that under your belt. Some of your choices border on illegal, but so far, no harm, no foul," Blake said in that deadpan way he had. "That Patience woman doesn't realize her son is the victim of a crime. He's not getting his appendix removed. I'll be able to find out about his condition and let you know."

"Thanks, Blake." I looked at him. For a second, he turned from the road and looked at me. Never getting more than a smirk from him, I nearly broke into tears again. He looked so worried about me. And maybe I saw something more there. Maybe, but my vision blurred with tears.

Of course, the timing couldn't be any worse. We were pulling up to the café. I didn't have any time to ask or say anything. Not that I knew what to ask or say. But I would have liked another few minutes alone with him. Instead, I opened the door.

"Thanks again, Blake. You are one in a million."

"I'll let you know what I find out."

I nodded, shut the car door, and headed into the café. Bea and Aunt Astrid were waiting.

❧ 4 ❧

LOVE HANDLES

"I can't believe that woman." Bea took my hands in hers. "You poor thing. I should have gone with you. We all know what kind of woman she is. What was I thinking, letting you go off by yourself?"

"It's okay, Bea." I wiped my nose with a scratchy napkin. "How were we to know she was going to switch her insanity to level eleven? But I don't know anything about Tom. I don't know what happened except that he was shot and that they took him in for emergency surgery right away."

"Maybe she was in shock," Bea offered, looking to her mother and me for validation. "No one, especially a mother, wants to get that phone call. That their son has been shot and is in the hospital. I know if I ever got that phone call, I'd be a basket case."

"That's true." I nodded.

"Let me make you some tea. I think some chamomile with extra honey is what you need. Plain and simple." Bea turned and started to work on her magic elixir. It wasn't really magic. It was just tea. But it sounded good.

"What do you think, Aunt Astrid? You've been kind of quiet," I said as I took a seat at my aunt's favorite table.

"Oh, I'm...thinking maybe Bea is right. Patience might be in shock. She might have said those same exact things to the doctor, had he shown up instead of you."

"I get the feeling you're trying to make me feel better." I folded my arms over my chest and leaned back in my chair.

"Well, I certainly don't want you to worry about what that woman said." She waved her hand lazily in front of her as if to shoo the insinuation of Patience's name. "Do you want to go home? Bea and I can handle the café."

"What would I do there?"

"I suspect you've got laundry and dishes." My aunt smirked.

"You know me too well," I replied with a tired smile. "What a morning." I rested my head in my hands.

"Here you go." Bea set a large paper cup next to me. It smelled flowery and sweet. The first sip was instantly calming.

"I'll work, Aunt Astrid. Blake said he'd find out what was happening with Tom." I took another sip. "He said since Tom was the victim of a crime, Patience wouldn't be able to keep him…"

I don't know what happened. The tears just started, and they wouldn't stop. My aunt took me in her arms and rocked me like I was a little girl. Bea dabbed her own eyes with a napkin, careful not to smear her makeup, and offered all kinds of encouragement.

"Don't upset yourself, Cath. Come on. Tom is exactly where he should be to get the help he needs. The doctors will fix him right up."

But that wasn't why I was crying. Sure, I was worried about Tom, and I was desperate to know that he was going to be all right. But I felt bad that I didn't feel as bad as I should have. Something was missing. When I looked up at my aunt, I could tell she knew. She could see right through me, literally and figuratively.

"What's wrong with me?" I whispered.

"Nothing, honey." She squeezed me tight. "Nothing at all."

Over the course of the day, I kept as busy as possible. When there weren't a lot of customers, I was in the back with Kevin Baker, our baker, wiping down the shelves and drawers and trying to stay out of his way while I organized the supplies and wrote down what inventory we were running out of. I even cleaned the bathroom, a chore I absolutely hated. Not because our bathroom was gross. On the contrary, I could sip coffee and eat a scone in our bathroom. That was how spotless it was. It just reminded me of the truck stop that was my bathroom at home.

Every time the phone rang, I'd stretch my neck to see if it was Blake or Jake calling to give us an update. Bea would turn and shake her head every time, so I'd just go back to what I was doing and try to forget why I was keeping to myself.

When it got to be five o'clock in the evening and we still had no word, I thought that Patience had really made good on her promise to ice us out.

"How can we not hear anything?" I grumbled. "Part of me wants to march down to that hospital and plant myself there until someone tells me something."

"I know it's frustrating," Aunt Astrid soothed. "But you know that woman is hoping you'll do just that. Don't give her the satisfaction."

"But don't you think Tom is going to be wondering where I am? If it were me, I'd expect to wake up and see him there." I wasn't lying. But I think my aunt knew that Blake popped into my mind first.

"Go home, Cath," Aunt Astrid ordered. "Take a hot shower. Put on your pajamas. Watch a couple old movies, and we'll see you tomorrow."

"Yes. That's a good idea. In fact, here." Bea grabbed a plastic container and scooped up a heaping helping of her spinach and pine nut salad along with some slices of bread and the last raspberry chocolate fig bar.

"Well, if I don't get any news, I'll at least have the healthiest colon in Wonder Falls," I scoffed.

"That's my Cath." Bea smiled as she handed me the takeout bag.

By the time I got out of the shower and into my jammies, Treacle was meowing at the kitchen window. He didn't say much after I told him about

Tom. He'd taken such a shine to him that I was sorry I'd even said anything.

We curled up in bed, and I snapped on the television, with the food Bea had sent me home with. I had a few bites, but my appetite wasn't there. By the time I'd gotten halfway through the movie, Treacle was sound asleep at the foot of the bed. I was wide-awake and had no interest in finding out who done it or if the couple lived happily ever after. I didn't even know what the movie was about.

So, with renewed energy, I started to do what I should have done days ago. I cleaned my house. Like the café, I did a deep cleaning. Shelves and junk drawers were not spared. Drawers and closets were tidied up. I even ventured into the fridge to throw away anything that had gone bad. By the time I was finished, there were four bags full of either junk I was going to donate or junk I was going to throw away.

When I finally got the coffee started and sat down at my kitchen table, I thought at least I got something accomplished. Still, there was no word on Tom. But at least my home felt cozy again.

The clock read three fifteen. I could get a cat nap in before it was time to get up for work. I snuggled into bed and quickly fell asleep next to Treacle, who had maneuvered himself to the center of the mattress.

I kept dreaming that I was waking up to Tom at the door. He was fine and kept saying he didn't get shot or that it wasn't serious. Over and over, I kept dreaming the same thing only to wake up in real life for a few short seconds and realize it was just a dream. That had to be my subconscious wishfully thinking for me.

But the last time I slipped into a dream and heard knocking on my door, I didn't want to answer it. There was something strange about it. I walked in a haze around my little house and hoped whoever it was would go away. Didn't they know if someone didn't answer, it meant they weren't home or didn't want to be bothered?

Finally, my eyes popped open, and I heard the very real knocking on my door.

Forgetting about Treacle next to me, I flung the covers aside and dashed to the front door. When I yanked it open, I hoped to see Tom, but instead it was Mrs. Kitt, my neighbor.

"I know. We have to quit meeting like this." She chuckled as if her morning visits were somehow cute. "I'm so sorry to bother you, honey. Yesterday it was cat food. Today, I'm hoping I can borrow a few spurts of window cleaner."

I didn't bother to hide my annoyance. After all, I'd only gotten a couple hours of fitful sleep.

"Window cleaner?" I had just used half a bottle cleaning the mirror in my bathroom. Somehow toothpaste spit had gotten to the very top of the slab over my sink.

"Thanks a million, hon. And if you could hurry. I've still got to get to work. You probably do too." She shifted from one foot to the other. Today she wasn't in her fuzzy pajamas but was instead wearing a rather tight skirt with a flowery blouse. To tell the truth, I liked her better in her floppy pj's.

"Yeah. I guess I do." I gave her a look before I muttered I'd be right back. When I came back, I caught her looking at her reflection in my windows, primping her hair and making those duck faces people on social media were always making. Was she on dope?

"Oh, thanks," she said as she took the window cleaner from me. When she turned to leave, I was sure she was going to say something like she'd have it back to me in a day or two or she'd buy me a new one or something.

"You might want to try taking a longer route to

work, if you are going to walk. It might help with those love handles. Bye!"

I looked behind me to see Treacle had gotten out of bed to see what the commotion was all about.

"Did you hear what she said?" I asked, watching her sashay past her house to the babe couple's house.

"I did. Did you smell alcohol on her breath?"

I shook my head no. "I ought to go give her a piece of my mind. Crazy old bed-headed biddy."

Instead I remembered I hadn't gotten a very good night's sleep and decided to let it go. I hopped in the shower and woke up a little more. The idea of walking with Bea didn't appeal to me today. I'd see her at the café, so I left a little early and walked there alone. As usual, Aunt Astrid was already inside.

"Did I miss anything after I left yesterday?" I asked.

"No, honey." Aunt Astrid tucked my hair behind my ears. "Did you get any sleep last night?"

"Not really. But my house is nice and clean, and all my laundry got done. Plus, if you need to use my bathroom, you can."

"I couldn't before?" Aunt Astrid tilted her head to the right.

"It was just a mess." I chuckled at her expression.

I was pleasantly surprised to see Jake had come with Bea this morning.

"You left without me," she pouted.

"I'm sorry. I just had a rough night and was feeling crabby. It isn't you. It's me." I patted Bea's hand.

"Well, we've got news. Tell her, Jake." Bea folded her hands and put them up to her chin. I looked up at him to see his expression wasn't joyful, but it wasn't forlorn either.

"Tom's surgery went well. He was under the knife for six hours. There is no way you would have been able to stay and wait for him all that time. So, it's a good thing you came home." He patted me on the shoulder. "Bea told me what Patience Warner said. I want you to put that out of your mind."

I nodded and waited for him to continue.

"He can't have visitors until they know he's out of the woods. He's really doped up, so he wouldn't know if you were there or not. Don't worry," he said.

"But he'll survive? He'll be okay?"

"That's what the doctor told me. So, just sit tight, and when the coast is clear, I'll make sure you can get in to see him."

"Thanks, Jake." I hugged him tightly. "That makes me feel better."

"But that isn't all," he said as he rubbed my back. "Patience has been there all night."

"That's to be expected," Bea soothed. "It's her son, after all."

"Yeah. Normally, I'd agree with you. But she was acting a little strange, even for a grieving mother."

I looked up and took a step back from Jake. This didn't sit well with me. When I looked at Aunt Astrid, I could tell that she was feeling edgy, too, about what Jake was saying.

"She was doing a lot of muttering to herself. Not just a comment about forgetting to pick up milk but more like an angry conversation with herself. Or someone we can't see." He chuckled but then regained his composure. "The doctor told me that when he told her Tom's status was improving, she didn't seem happy. He thought for a minute she was on drugs, the way her eyes kept flitting back and forth. But she took her seat in the waiting room and demanded that the doctor send for her when Tom was in his private room."

"Someone should suggest that woman have a psych evaluation," I muttered. "When do you think I'll be able to see him?"

Jake said that Tom was going to be kept under surveillance in the intensive care unit for about five days. Then he'd be moved to a regular room.

"At that time, I'm going to question him about what happened. His mother probably won't want to stay for that. I'll call you as soon as she's gone."

"That sounds risky. Will it get you in trouble, Jake? If there is a chance you could get busted, it isn't worth it. I'll just wait until he can walk into the café on his own," I said.

"No. And if it turns out that we can't get her away for a half an hour or so, I'll make sure I tell him what's happening so he knows why you aren't there. No one talks to my cousin-in-law like that and gets away with it." He winked at me. "Besides, she's got to eat and change clothes at some time."

It was a weight off my shoulders that Tom made it through surgery. I was glad and thought that maybe his mother would feel that same relief. Maybe she'd even say she was sorry to me for behaving the way she did. It was possible.

FOR THE NEXT COUPLE OF DAYS, I WAITED

for Jake to give me a call or tell me that today was the day I'd be able to stop by.

Finally, I got an update from Jake one morning at the café. He told me that Patience has been at her son's bedside morning, noon, and night and had yet to change her clothes. Jake hadn't questioned Tom yet because he was still on heavy medication.

I took a deep breath and kissed my cat's head before setting him on the windowsill. A couple of regulars stroked his fur as he arched his back up high, purring happily at the extra attention.

"I can't worry about it," I said. "He's made it through surgery, and it sounds like he is out of the woods. They'd have said something if he were in any kind of trouble."

"That's right," Jake assured me. "I'd like to stick around, but I've got to get back to work. I left Blake with all the paperwork."

My heart jumped at the sound of his name. I wondered why he hadn't come by since that day at the hospital. But if I put myself in his shoes, I'd probably stay away too. No one wants to be the third wheel.

Bea gave Jake some food to take back to the police station, and of course, they kissed and giggled and held hands like the ship was going down before he finally left.

"What do you think about all this, Aunt Astrid?" I asked.

"Yeah, Mom. You've been kind of quiet whenever Patience Warner's name comes up. What do you think is wrong with her?"

Aunt Astrid was remaining rather tight-lipped. It was something that happened to her whenever Patience was the topic of discussion. It was like she was stacking crystal goblets, one on top of the other, and any sudden move could send the whole thing crashing down.

"I've felt a crowded sensation whenever her name is mentioned," my aunt said. "Like someone or something is trying to push me in a corner, but it's not strong enough to do it...yet."

"Do you think that she...?" I suddenly lost my train of thought. Treacle looked up from my arms toward the door. His fur went straight up, and he growled way deep down inside.

"What is it, Treacle?"

"That's bad. Very bad." He pulled his head and neck closer to me. His claws came out instinctively and poked my arms.

"Hello, Astrid," Mrs. Kitt sneered at my aunt. She didn't look anything like the nice older lady who had been my quiet, homebody neighbor for so many years. I couldn't understand why she looked like a completely different person.

ST. JOSEPH HOSPITAL

"Hello, Dorothy?" My aunt looked as if some dude wearing nothing but a raincoat had opened it wide.

"Mrs. Kitt?" I let Treacle hop out of my arms and scurry under one of the tables. I was as shocked as Aunt Astrid was. "Wow. You look so different."

Bea just stood and tried not to stare as she took my neighbor's order.

"Just give me one of those mint teas, and I'll take an orange-and-poppy scone to go," Mrs. Kitt said, leaning over the counter as if she were trying to read the fine print of a contract. It was a rather provocative pose, but I didn't say anything. Mainly because what could I say? *Hey, Mrs. Kitt, your cans are almost showing?*

47

It had only been about a week since Mrs. Kitt had come bumbling to my door, asking for cat food. Now, she was wearing a skirt that, if it reached her knees, was long and a stretchy top that plunged daringly low, revealing some kind of lacy thing underneath that barely concealed her cleavage.

Her hair was still lopsided, and some of the gray roots were coming in. Her makeup was a little heavy for this early in the daytime, but she seemed to be comfortable. In fact, she acted downright conceited.

Bea handed Mrs. Kitt her tea and scone along with her change and wished her a pleasant day. In return, she got a once-over from the woman and an eye roll.

"Dorothy, you look so different," my aunt said gently. "Are you doing okay?"

Mrs. Kitt looked at my aunt like she was noticing something gross floating on top of the water of a pool.

"Of course I am. I've never been better." She didn't even attempt to straighten her skirt to maybe get a millimeter more covering her legs. "I've been doing a little bit of dieting and working out. You know, you and your daughter could do with some improvements yourselves."

"What?" Bea finally spoke.

"Don't get upset, dearie," Mrs. Kitt snapped without even looking at Bea. "I'm just being honest."

"Well, we'll take your suggestion to heart." Aunt Astrid waved to Bea, who looked like she was ready to climb over the counter and tackle Mrs. Kitt. "Good day, Dorothy."

Mrs. Kitt admired her reflection in just about every surface then turned and left without saying another word.

"That is not my neighbor." I pointed, with my mouth hanging open. "Mrs. Kitt is a nice older lady with baggy clothes and a nice yard with flowers, who never bothers anyone. Not Mrs. Bouncy Galore and her two-ton ego."

"You know, I've heard of people losing weight and starting to get healthy who transform into nasty, snobby know-it-alls because they are suddenly getting the attention they were craving," Bea said with a frown. "That doesn't give her the right to be so rude."

"I don't know about you guys, but I don't think she's lost any weight since I saw her last week," I interrupted. "She doesn't look like she's working out either. She looks like she just slapped on some hooker-wear and called it a day."

"Maybe she's going through a phase," Aunt

Astrid said calmly. "She's been a widow for ten years. Sometimes our own mortality can hit us in a way we don't expect."

I noticed Treacle emerging from beneath one of the tables by the window. He hopped up on the ledge and watched as Mrs. Kitt sashayed past.

"What do you make of it?" I asked my cat.

"There was something following her."

"Something we need to worry about?"

"I don't know."

"Hey, Bea. Did you pick up on anything from Mrs. Kitt?"

"Besides a severe case of bad manners?" Bea snapped. "Yeah, I noticed a slight shadow, but I don't think it was anything more than her newly developed *confidence*." She made air quotes with her fingers.

"Don't let her get to you, Bea." I took a deep breath. "She told me the same thing when she stopped by my house."

"You didn't say anything about that," Aunt Astrid said.

"I don't think I told you guys she came back, asking for some glass cleaner. This was after the day she'd asked for the cat food," I said.

"Glass cleaner?" Bea asked.

"Don't ask me." I shrugged. "Who knows what she finds relaxing? Maybe cleaning the windows of the babe couple's house is fun for her."

"Girls." Aunt Astrid shook her head. "She's alone. She has no children. We don't know what kind of life she's lived. Cath, you just got through saying that in all the years you've lived next door to her, you've barely talked to her."

"Yes, but I'm not a good example. I never talk to anyone but you guys. It's my nature. I'm an introvert." I put my hands on my hips and looked seriously at my aunt. "Besides, she obviously had lengthy conversations with the babe couple because they asked her to watch their cats while they are on vacation. So see? She's talking to one neighbor, but she's ignoring me. Until she needs something. Then I'm her best friend. That's called manipulation."

"Do you sit up at night, rationalizing your weird quirks so you can rattle them off like this when the opportunity presents itself?" Bea asked.

"When I have neighbors who don't visit me, what else is there to do?" I asked.

"There's something wrong with her," Treacle insisted.

"You think so?" I asked him and watched as he stared down the street, his eyes not blinking and his ears flat against his head.

"Yes."

I agreed with Treacle but chalked it up to some kind of female midlife crisis. Even if she was a little bit past midlife. She wasn't hurting anyone either.

THAT NIGHT I REALIZED I HAD THOUGHT about Mrs. Kitt more than I had Tom.

"I'm breaking my own heart, Treacle," I said as I made myself some macaroni and cheese at the stove. "I feel like I've been trying to gently dump myself and I'm not getting the hint."

"Do you think talking to Tom might make things better?" he asked, slinking up to me.

"I don't know. I don't know if he's conscious. If he isn't, it would probably be the best time to spill my guts." I shrugged.

"You'd never do that." Treacle wound his body around mine and purred as he looked right in my face. *"You still care about him."*

"I do. I really do." I ran my hand over Treacle's fur. "I just don't feel *that* way about him."

"The way you feel about Blake?"

"What?"

"Come on, Cath. You know he's the guy that always

caught your attention. He's the complete opposite of you. He is by the book. You make it up as you go along. He's just the facts. You are all about the what-ifs. You're perfect for each other."

"And you've been wise to this for how long?" I stopped petting him and folded my arms over my chest.

"Are you joking?" He nudged me with his head, hoping for more scratches behind the ears. I wasn't budging. *"Marshmallow, Peanut Butter, and I have had lengthy discussions about it."*

"Oh really?"

I wasn't sure how I felt about my aunt Astrid's familiar, Marshmallow, and Bea's familiar, Peanut Butter, talking about me with my familiar. It was rather troubling. Sort of like having family members trying to fix me up on a date with a cousin of a friend just because he's single. Not because he'd be a good match.

"We think that it would heighten your gifts if you had the challenge of a man who had such a firm grasp in this world and not the paranormal. You see how it works for Bea."

Treacle sat up straight, looking like the statues of cats in Egyptian hieroglyphics. Then he yawned.

"Bea and Jake are the exception. Those two get all

lovey-dovey over a sneeze. I'm not like that, and neither is Blake."

"And that's what makes it so perfect."

I rubbed my forehead because I felt a headache coming on. I ate my macaroni and cheese, washed my face, and put the television on. For the second night, I really didn't watch the movie. Due to that darn cat, I couldn't get Blake out of my mind. I was a mess.

Throughout the night, I kept waking up. It was a sign that something was going on that was disrupting the normal flow of energy. At least, that was what Bea told me. So, at one o'clock in the morning, I got dressed and decided to go to the hospital and see if I couldn't sweet-talk my way onto the floor Tom was on.

When I went outside, there was movement out of the corner of my eye that made me freeze and listen.

Someone or something was moving about. I was in the glow of my porch light. The thought of a bull's-eye hanging around my neck crossed my mind. But it turned out the sound was coming from the direction of Mrs. Kitt's house. Footsteps. They were walking away in the direction of the babe couple's house.

"She probably forgot to feed the cats in her haste

to rip the tags off her new outfit from Hoochie Mamas," I muttered before getting into my car.

As I sat in the driver's seat, I looked around before turning on the engine. No shadow people or mud monsters or anything else that nightmares were made of lurking about. It was a cool night and nothing more.

The drive to the hospital was pleasant. There were no cars on the road at this hour. It was nice to be out when the world was asleep. I felt like I was doing something I shouldn't, something that would be my secret alone. Well, Treacle knew where I was headed, but I knew my secrets were safe with him.

St. Joseph Hospital was a big place, and the emergency entrance was bustling. I drove around the building and found a quiet parking spot in the regular visitors' area.

Visiting hours were from eight in the morning until five o'clock in the evening. There was going to be a problem convincing anyone at the information desk to let me in to see Tom.

There had to be a way to distract the front desk for a few seconds while I slipped into the elevator banks. They wouldn't see me there.

Before I went into the slowly revolving door that was big enough to accommodate a wheelchair, two walkers, and myself, I looked around outside. There were cameras all over the place, so throwing something through a window wasn't my best idea.

Aunt Astrid could shift the air around her and camouflage herself. She could walk right up to the desk, do a dance, and they'd never see her.

"There is no use complaining who has a better gift when it comes to sneaking into places, Cath. Just figure it out."

So, I put a call out. Any animals within the area might be able to help me out. As it was, a squirrel and a blue jay came to my aid. I spoke slowly and carefully with them, explaining I'd need them to cause a real distraction.

The blue jay was happy to help, as he used a colorful array of words I didn't think birds even knew. Like I said, they communicated like drunken sailors.

The squirrel was a bit more refined.

His reply was simply, "*All right.*"

I suggested they slowly and quietly slip into the revolving door and, when it opened into the lobby, just fly around and scurry over a few feet. I would enter through the handicap door, and it would stay open for a minute or two. Once they'd gotten everyone's attention, they could scoot back out and be home before dawn.

The squirrel agreed. I wouldn't repeat what the blue jay said, but he too essentially agreed.

I watched them slink into the revolving door and slowly inch their way along the treaded mat until the door opened into the lobby. It was like a gun went off.

Just as I hit the button, making the handicap door slowly yawn open, the blue jay began to caw and shriek as he dove at the man sitting at the information desk. The squirrel did one better, scurrying halfway up the pant leg of the security guard who was also standing at the information desk. There were several folks sleeping in the lobby and a few more milling around who also began to shout and squeal as nature infiltrated their space.

The blue jay and the squirrel made good on their agreement and pulled everyone's attention away from the elevator banks and me. They swooped and scampered and made all kinds of racket as the people watched and climbed on chairs while ducking and covering their heads. I should have known it would happen, but before I slipped into the hallway with the elevator banks, I saw that blue jay poop on the information desk.

"Get out before the door closes!" I shouted tele-pathically.

Both the bird and the squirrel froze and looked in the same direction. Within seconds, they were bolting to the door that was slowly closing on its own. As quickly as they'd gotten inside the lobby, they slipped out.

I let out a deep sigh and stepped into the first elevator, pressing the button for the third floor and the intensive care unit. I wasn't sure what I was going to say when I got there. I just thought I'd act like I belonged and see how far I could get. It didn't take long for me to realize that I wasn't going to get far at all. Not because any of the staff thought I looked out of place but because Patience was there.

❦ 6 ❧

MAN WITHOUT A FACE

I stepped off the elevator and quietly walked around, attempting to casually look into the rooms for a glimpse of Tom. I didn't know what his room number was. I couldn't ask. So I winged it. When I rounded the nurses' station that was abandoned at the moment, that was when I saw her.

Patience Warner was standing at the window that looked into Tom's room, with a man dressed in black standing next to her. He looked even more out of place than I did. If I hadn't known any better, his black suit and tie and black fedora would have made me think he was an undertaker. But as I looked closer, I saw that he literally had no face.

I pulled myself back and stood against the wall,

wondering if it was just fatigue. Maybe I was more tired than I thought, and this was just a hallucination. There was part of me that wanted to look again, but an overwhelming sense of dread swept over me, and I couldn't move.

Where were the nurses? Where were the doctors on the night shift? Hospitals were quieter at night, I knew that, but this was deserted. Now I really regretted making the decision to come here.

It's just the hospital. All the energy and worry and sickness are overloading your senses. If you look again, you'll see the man is just weird looking but not faceless, I tried to encourage myself.

I hadn't realized I was holding my breath. I let it out slowly, took two more deep inhales to calm myself, and peeked around the corner.

I wished I would have just gone back home. No. I wished I never would have come out tonight at all.

Patience was standing in the middle of the hallway, facing me. The man in black wasn't there anymore. If he went into Tom's room or another patient's room, I didn't know. But she was standing there, staring at me.

She didn't move. She didn't say anything. But as I looked at her, I was able to discern that she hadn't changed her clothes since the day when I saw her. Her hands were clenching and unclenching at her sides. And perhaps the worst part was her lips were moving, saying something that made her snarl and grimace as she said it. Her voice wasn't louder than a whisper. I went to speak, hoping to break her trance, when one of the nurses came bustling back to the station and took a seat, her back to me.

The familiar sound of her rolling chair, her fingers tapping on the keyboard of her computer, and a few pings and dings from patients' rooms and the elevator brought normalcy back.

When I looked back at Patience, she was just five feet away and staring at me with icy eyes. I didn't want to talk. She could take it up with security and the police that I had made it onto the floor.

Quickly, I went back the way I came. It wouldn't have surprised me one bit if Patience was following after me, mumbling her crazy, and ready to corner me in an empty elevator car where she could step in and slash me to pieces with a scalpel she stole from some surgery room.

Thankfully, that was just my imagination. I got into the elevator alone, and the doors closed immediately. My stomach flipped as the elevator descended to the lobby, and I walked out as if nothing was the matter. But I ran to my car, and once I was inside, I locked the doors.

Thankfully, no one was on the road. I pushed the boundary of breaking the speed limit and was home within minutes.

I shut off my lights before pulling into the driveway. For some reason, I thought that was rather stealthy. As soon as I turned the car off, I had my house key in my hand and dashed through the front door as quickly as possible and slammed the door shut behind me. I slipped the dead bolt into place, followed by the chain lock.

"What happened?" Treacle asked as he stretched his paws in front of him and his backside up in the air.

"I don't know," I replied. "All I know is that I shouldn't have gone over there."

I went to my room and snapped on the television. The sound of Jimmy Stewart's voice as he spoke in one of those westerns he was in was like an old friend even though I didn't like westerns. It brought calm to my house instead of the freakiness I'd just escaped.

I slipped into bed after checking all the windows to make sure the house was locked up tight. Crazy as it seemed, I wasn't so much afraid of the man in black showing up as I was Patience.

Sleep came quickly, and when I woke up, my house looked pretty in the bright light of day. I'd overslept. Within seconds of realizing it, there was pounding on the door.

"Let me guess!" I shouted as Treacle lay still on the bed. "You need to borrow a bottle of shampoo." I snorted as I yanked open the door, expecting to see Mrs. Kitt standing there.

"What? I have plenty of shampoo," Bea said. "My gosh, what happened to you? You run a marathon this morning?"

"Yeah. I'm secretly training. I eat cheeseburgers and onion rings to keep you off my scent until I'm ready to announce my Olympic run." I walked away from the door, leaving it open for Bea to come in.

"You okay to come to work?" she asked.

"I don't know. Smell me." I leaned toward my cousin. She took a whiff and shrugged.

"You smell okay to me."

"Then, yes, I'm coming to work. Give me a second to throw on some clothes and brush my teeth."

"Hey, did you go out last night?" Bea asked as she leaned against the closed bathroom door.

"I did. You won't believe what I tried to do." I told her about my help from the little woodland creatures and my encounter in the IC unit.

"No face?" Bea bit her thumbnail. "Those kinds of guys are often seen at hospitals."

"Yeah, but that can't be good. A guy with no face dressed like he works for the IRS isn't what most people say angels look like. In fact, they'd probably say that's more like their hooved, fork-tongued, pointy-tailed, horned opposites. If you catch my meaning."

I turned on the faucet to wash my face and brush my teeth.

"As for how she reacted to you, well, that's creepy." Bea folded her arms. "She's not a nice lady. I wouldn't be surprised if she were just so mad you were there that she couldn't speak."

"No. There was more to it than that." I pulled the door open, wearing my robe, and grabbed a new pair of jeans and a fresh T-shirt.

"You are so lucky," Bea said out of the blue.

"I'm lucky? About what?"

"You can just get dressed, throw on jeans and a T-shirt, pull your hair back, and look like a million bucks." She shook her head. "Not everyone can do that. I won't even get the mail without at least a little lip gloss on."

"You are smoking crack again, aren't you?" I smirked as I shimmied into my pants and grabbed my Converse All-Star gym shoes.

"No. I mean it. If you saw what I see and what Tom sees, maybe you'd be a little more…I don't know."

"Normal?"

"No. You'll never be that."

"Happy?"

"I wouldn't recognize you happy. No, you'd be more awesome than you already are." Bea smiled since she made me laugh.

I shook my head and grabbed my keys as we headed out the door with Treacle scooting out just as it closed. He walked with us along the sidewalk. His head swung low as he scanned the neighborhood, and his tail waved languidly back and forth.

"Hey, when you were out last night, did you see Mrs. Kitt?" Bea asked as we started walking toward the café.

"I heard her walking around about one in the morning. At least I think it was her. The sound was going that way. I figured she was going to the babe couple's house."

"Can you quit calling them that? They have names. It's Turk and—"

"Yes, Turk and Renee Lourdes. That's even more embarrassing than the babe couple." I shivered. "Who names their kid Turk?"

"I don't know, but they are a sweet couple who are very affectionate." Bea harrumphed. "I don't see anything wrong with that."

"Well, of course you don't." I laughed. "You and Jake are a close second in the PDA awards."

"We like our public displays of affection."

"I should hope so." I slipped my arm through Bea's and pulled her to my side. "This is about as affectionate as I'll get in public. So, tell me, why did you ask if I saw Mrs. Kitt?"

"She was out in her yard last night. Peanut Butter was meowing at the window. I didn't know what his problem was." She gestured with her free hand. "I thought maybe there was a cricket or a moth on the window driving him nuts. So when I looked, I saw Mrs. Kitt standing outside."

"What was she doing?"

"Staring at the house?" Bea looked at me.

"Whose house?"

"My house." She frowned. "What do you think

that is all about? She wasn't acting crazy or anything."

"No, she was just standing in her yard in the middle of the night, staring at your front door. That's not acting crazy."

"Oh, come on, Cath. Don't freak me out. She's been acting strange, and I'm worried about her. Like you said, she's just a nice old widow. If she's losing her marbles, we should help."

I started to chuckle.

"What's so funny?" Bea asked.

"You said 'if she's losing her marbles.'" I started to laugh harder. "That's the kind of socially unacceptable thing I'd say."

"You're a bad influence, Cath Greenstone."

"Me? I'm not the one suggesting she be sized for a straitjacket." I laughed even harder.

"I didn't say that. That's not funny." The fact that Bea was trying not to laugh made me laugh even harder. Sure, it was inappropriate and perhaps a smidge juvenile to talk this way, but I couldn't help it. It made me feel like a kid when saying something we weren't supposed to was so deliciously fun.

"Has your mom noticed anything about the house or Mrs. Kitt?" I asked once I regained my composure.

"I don't know. But Mrs. Kitt isn't herself." Bea sighed.

"I concur." I looked down at Treacle, who was glancing over his shoulder, back at the house.

"What's the matter?" I asked Treacle without moving my lips.

"I think I hear something."

"Why don't you go explore and see if the babe couple's cats have seen anything? Have you ever talked with them before?"

"No," Treacle said, reminding me that they were indoor cats. *"But I'll go peek in the windows and see what I can. I'll let you know."*

"Be careful, and make sure you are home before dark." I got a hearty meow in return.

I turned back to Bea. "Treacle will do a little snooping for us."

"Mom is going to wonder why we are so late," Bea said. "We better hurry."

"I'll tell her it was your fault." I let go of Bea's arm so we could quicken our pace. "If you weren't making fun of people with mental issues, we would have been there sooner."

"Oh, just wait. Wait until Tom comes into the café. It will take you three days to recover from the embarrassment I'm going to cause."

"Good luck getting him in the café. His mother isn't going to let him anywhere near the place."

I couldn't help but think if anyone really did need to be fitted for a straitjacket, it was Patience. She was dangerous. I didn't know how, and I certainly didn't know why. But my gut said it. And Blake always told me to trust my gut.

❧ 7 ❧

ANIMAL RESCUE

The day went by without any real excitement until the noontime rush. Mrs. Kitt showed up again. I never wore stretch pants or yoga pants. To me, they were just a little too revealing, and I was already in my thirties. Mrs. Kitt was twice my age, and let me just say, I would be sticking to my initial opinion on stretch pants.

Even if Mrs. Kitt was working out and dieting like she said, she had a long way to go. This was not a good look for her. She looked cheap and beat-up, like she'd had a hard night on the corner in the red-light district.

"Hello, Bea," she said as if she were about to pick a fight.

"Hi, Mrs. Kitt," Bea said, attempting to touch the woman's hand and get a reading from her. "How are you doing today?"

"I think you better just cut out the small talk," Mrs. Kitt said.

I watched my aunt get up and slowly walk to Bea's side. "Is there a problem, Dorothy?" Aunt Astrid asked.

"Yeah. There is a problem. That hussy of a daughter of yours. What does she think she's doing looking out her window in the middle of the night, wearing a negligee?"

"Negligee? I was wearing Jake's XXL Wonder Falls PD shirt." She wrinkled her face. "And, Mrs. Kitt, what are you doing looking in my windows?"

Good point, I thought.

"Don't think for a second I don't know what you are up to. You aren't half the woman you think you are. I'll have that husband of yours, and I'll have this café too. Just wait. And when I do, I'll burn them both."

"What?" Bea exploded. "What are you talking about?"

"Dorothy, something is obviously bothering you. Come with me." My aunt tried to lead her to the back of the café, where she did her psychic readings, but Mrs. Kitt yanked her arm away.

"All right, folks," I said to the gawkers sitting in their seats. "Don't stare, now. This isn't the Friday-night fights. Come on."

But no one was going to look away when Mrs. Kitt was making a spectacle of herself and Bea.

"I'll burn them both." She looked Bea up and down, and all I could think of was Darla Castellano.

"Oh my gosh!" I gasped as soon as Mrs. Kitt left.

I hurried to Bea, who was near tears. She was the nicest one of all of us Greenstones. It was her gift that people talked to her, opened up to her. Rarely did she ever have anyone attack her personally like Mrs. Kitt just did. It obviously had her rattled.

"Go on in the back, Bea. I'll handle things up here," I said as I slipped behind the counter. "Okay, folks. The only thing more surprising at the Brew-Ha-Ha Café than the food is some of our customers. Okay, everyone, enjoy your food and coffee, and what can I get for you, sir?" I asked the next person in line.

Bea and her mom were in the back for a little over ten minutes. When she finally came back out, I could tell that Bea had been crying.

"It's okay." I rubbed her arm. "Mrs. Kitt's obviously suffering from something. Maybe I'll stop by her house and see if there is someone who I can get in touch with who can help her."

"Why would she say those things about Jake and me?" Bea asked, looking embarrassed.

"I don't know." I shrugged. "But rest assured, you've had worse things said about you by better people than her."

Bea started to chuckle and bumped me with her hip.

"Leave it to you, Cath."

"I'm just putting things in perspective." I pinched her behind.

"You did. You always know just what to say."

The rest of the day went by without a hitch. There was no crazed Mrs. Kitt cruising the place, and I also didn't hear any news about Tom. No news was good news.

"I'll call Jake if you want me to and see if he's heard anything," Bea offered.

"No." I focused on stuffing the napkin dispensers. "I'm sure if anything went south, he'd call. Besides, Tom needs to rest if he's going to get out of there in another day or two."

As the sun started to set, Treacle came in through the open back door. Kevin Baker often left it open when he had all three ovens going. Treacle would slink in and out as he pleased. But this time he was running and screaming my name.

"What? What's the matter?" I asked as he hopped up on the counter to look directly at me.

"I went to the house on the other side of Mrs. Kitt's place."

"What happened?"

"The cats are starving. They said they haven't been fed in a week. Maybe more."

"Oh no!" I looked at Bea and Aunt Astrid. Quickly, I repeated what Treacle said and went to the phone. "I'll call Old Murray and tell him to meet us there."

Old Murray Willis ran the animal rescue in town. He was a sweet old fellow who had brought Treacle and me together when Treacle was a kitten barely able to see straight. There were many times I'd stop by the shelter with extra dog and cat food if I saw it on sale, and they were always in need of rags and towels. I liked to help because of the fact I found that I liked animals a lot more than most people.

Within just a few minutes, Murray was at the house with Bea and me.

"Should we break it down?" I asked, clenching

my fists and taking a Bruce Lee stance as if I were ready to kick in the door.

"Maybe we should try knocking first?" Bea suggested.

"Yeah. Okay. If you want to play it safe." I shrugged.

"I do," she replied as she pounded on the door. There was no answer but the pitiful cries of the cats inside pacing back and forth in front of the door.

"Oh no. Don't cry!" I used my mind to try and get through to them. *"We're here to help. We'll help you. Just hold on a little longer."*

"Ain't no one home? That's typical," Old Murray growled. "I ain't waitin' for no police. I'll call Blake. He won't mind if I crack a window or two."

"Just because he volunteers at the shelter doesn't mean that you can bust into a house, Murray." I patted him on the arm. "Just hold on a few more minutes."

I waved Bea over and jerked my head toward Mrs. Kitt's house. "How about it? Want to knock on her door?"

"We have no choice." Bea pinched her lips together.

"Okay, I'll stand in front. You wait off to the side. That way she'll have to go through me to get to you.

That ought to give three solid seconds' lead time to run away."

"You're such a help, Cath."

"I do what I can." We walked across the yard to Mrs. Kitt's front door. Even with her weird new sense of style and her nasty disposition, Mrs. Kitt's front porch was clean and welcoming. So welcoming that when I went to knock on the door, it opened right up.

"That's not good," Bea said, leaning back slightly.

I gave the door a push, and it opened all the way.

"Hello? Mrs. Kitt? It's Cath Greenstone from next door! Are you home?" I listened but didn't hear anything. "I'm coming in, Mrs. Kitt! It's just me and my cousin." I nodded, pleased with myself for not revealing right off the bat that Bea was with me.

"I don't hear anything," Bea said. We stepped inside the house. It was dark and stuffy. Before my eyes could adjust, I stepped on something crunchy. Freezing like I was on a tightrope, I looked down to see shards of broken mirror.

"Uh oh," I muttered. "Don't come in any farther, Bea. This looks like trouble."

"What kind of trouble?" she asked.

"The bad kind? How do I know what kind of trouble? Trouble is trouble, right?"

I looked around without moving and saw a set of keys on the table next to the door. It had a huge key ring of two hearts with a gaudy ribbon through them. There was only one key on the chain. It had to be for the babe couple's house. I snatched it up and tossed it to Bea as she stood on the porch.

"See if that opens the front door of the *Lourdeses'* house," I said. "Did you see that? I didn't call them the babe couple?"

Quickly, after rolling her eyes, Bea went next door, and I heard her and Old Murray get the door open. I took just a few steps farther inside, staying on tiptoe so as not to contaminate the crime scene.

Of course, I didn't know if it was a crime scene. But a door left open, a shattered mirror, and then the body of Mrs. Kitt lying in the bathroom...

"Oh no!" I cried and dashed over to her. The mirrors in the bathroom had been smashed too. "Mrs. Kitt? Mrs. Kitt? Can you hear me?" I called before I got to her. But I soon realized that she didn't hear me. Her eyes stared straight up, with a look of terror on her face. But if that wasn't weird enough, she was wearing the strangest clothes. An exercise outfit about three sizes too small. Her makeup was garish and all over her face. What had she been doing? Or thinking?

"Bea! You better call 911!" I shouted.

I backtracked carefully to the front door and jumped onto the porch. I was pretty sure that I didn't touch anything but the keys. Bea was hurrying back across the lawn with the keys in her hand.

"Old Murray's got the cats, the poor things. He said they are very weak and dehydrated."

"Oh no. Well, if anyone can fix them up, it'll be Old Murray." I pointed into the dark house. "Mrs. Kitt's in there."

Bea squared her shoulders like she was ready for a confrontation.

"She's dead." I grimaced.

"Dead? We just saw her today. She was alive and kicking." Bea's eyes bulged from their sockets.

"I'd guess maybe a heart attack. But what do I know? Usually people who have heart attacks don't shatter all the mirrors in their house first." I looked around for a phone. "And they don't dress up like they are in some nineteen eighties rock video."

"What in the world are you talking about?" Bea asked.

"Go take a look before they wheel her out of here," I said. "But I don't think we better walk around too much. Let's call from my house."

The 911 operator had just hung up when we heard the sirens getting closer.

"I can't believe this. She was just in the café ranting and raving, and now she's..." Bea slid her finger across her neck.

"Before the fuzz shows up, let's go look in the babe couple's house," I suggested, bouncing my eyebrows up and down.

"What in the world for?"

"I'd like to see what the inside of their house looks like," I admitted. But something had me wondering if maybe there wasn't something else going on in Turk and Renee Lourdes's home.

8

SMASHING MIRRORS

"It's just a normal house," Bea said as she followed behind me. "What do you think you are going to find in there?"

"I don't know," I said. "They're just so weird in public I'd like to know what their house looks like."

"They don't act any different than Jake and me." Bea lifted her chin.

"Right, and look at the house of oddities you call home." I chuckled.

"You are off your rocker. There isn't anything wrong with my house."

"I didn't say there was. Especially if you like hearts and 'I love you' plaques and kissing angels and basset hounds and sea anemones. It's like the house where St. Valentine is embarrassed to go."

"It's not that bad, and you know it." She smiled.

"No. Your house is lovely. It's like my home away from home," I replied as we carefully pushed the door open to the Lourdeses' estate. We stepped inside and listened. There was no sound at all. The smell of cat litter that hadn't been changed in a while was in the air. That made me feel bad. Those poor cats.

"Did Old Murray check the house for any other animals?"

"No. He scooped up the two that were at the door and left," Bea said, looking around. "This place isn't what I expected. It looks like a showroom floor display of furniture and pictures."

"Yeah, and it's absolutely spotless. Wait." I gasped. "Would you look at this?"

"What is it?"

"Their wedding picture." I clapped my hand over my mouth and started to laugh. "Can you get any sappier than this?" I held up the picture of the babe couple. Renee was in her white dress looking adoringly into Turk's eyes. She had her hand on his cheek, and he had his chin up but his eyes down. "It looks like the cover of a Harlequin Romance."

"You really are too much, Cath. Put that down. I thought we were looking for sick or wounded animals." Bea walked into the living room ahead of me.

"You're right. I'm going to go upstairs, and you can cover this floor, and together we'll check the basement." I didn't wait for a reply and quickly ran up the steps to the second level. There were four photos of the couple on the walls. They were pretty but just a little too sweet for my taste. I was sad to report back to Bea that there wasn't anything out of the ordinary upstairs except an overwhelming number of mirrors around. It wasn't like some swinger's pad. But the place was big enough. The illusion of space was unnecessary.

"Did you find anything?" I asked Bea, who was looking at one of the mirrors in the living room. It was a pretty, full-length looking glass with an elegant rolling scroll around the edges. It matched the swirls in the fabric of their furniture.

When Bea didn't reply, I asked her again, startling her.

"What? Oh, no. I don't see anything out of the ordinary in here."

"Let's check the basement. The police will be at Mrs. Kitt's house any minute." We both hurried through the kitchen and down some steps to a door that led to the basement.

"Unbelievable." I sighed. "A home gym? How corny."

"They just want to stay in shape," Bea defended.

"Yeah, gross." I took her hand as we went back up the steps to the kitchen. "Looks like there were only two cats. That's a relief. I'll go to Old Murray's later to check on them."

"That's a good idea," Bea said absently.

"Are you all right?"

"Yeah, Cath. Why don't you go greet the police? I'll close things up here." She looked toward the living room.

"Um, okay. Don't stay in here too long. This place is creepy in its normalcy." I walked out of the house just as the police were getting out of the car in Mrs. Kitt's driveway.

It was seconds before a black-and-white car followed by a familiar sedan pulled up with an ambulance in the driveway. I waved to Jake and Blake, who strolled up to me. No one was in a hurry. Mrs. Kitt's condition wasn't going to change.

"How did you know something was wrong?" Jake asked. I was about to tell him that Treacle told me but caught myself before sounding like a total loon.

"She'd borrowed some cat food from me, and I didn't realize I'd given her my last can," I lied. "I went to borrow a can back from her and found the door open."

It wasn't my greatest fabrication. And I could tell by Jake's face that he thought there might be a little more to it, but he declined pushing the issue.

Blake had walked into the house with the EMTs and was out again by the time I finished talking to Jake.

"Where's Bea?" he asked.

"She's still next door. We went and checked if there were more than two cats. She should have been out of there by now," I muttered.

"I'll go get her," Jake said before crossing the grass and going into the neighbor's house. In just a minute, they were coming back out, and Bea looked upset. Jake went into Mrs. Kitt's house without saying another word.

"Are you all right?" I whispered. Perhaps she and Jake had a spat. Maybe he scolded her about going into the house. I would smooth it over and take the heat for it. It was my idea after all.

"I'm fine." She didn't look at me when she spoke. Instead, her eyes focused on the open door to Mrs. Kitt's house. "Have they gotten her out yet?"

"Not yet." I folded my arms and shifted from one foot to the other. "I wonder why the mirrors were broken. You know what I bet it is? In a lot of those true-crime stories, serial killers don't want to see themselves, especially when they are doing the act." I motioned my hand like I were stabbing someone in a shower. "Mrs. Kitt was probably murdered by one of those psychos who has an issue seeing his own reflection. So he smashed them all."

I rocked back and forth on my heels and waited for Bea's response.

"You're probably right," she muttered.

"You think so?"

"Yeah. Cath, I'm not feeling well. I'm going to go home." She didn't wait for my reply before heading to her house that was across the street and down a couple houses. All I could think was that maybe this had upset her more than she wanted me to know. Maybe she picked up on something sad or out of line.

When Blake came out of the house, he looked around, saw me, and headed right over.

"So? What's the verdict?" I asked.

"Looks like a heart attack," he said and went into some details about how the blood vessels reacted and how the person could collapse without knowing what was happening and blah, blah, blah.

"Yeah. What about all the smashed mirrors?" I

put my hands on my hips before repeating my theory about a serial killer on the loose.

"We won't know for sure until after the autopsy."

"The mirror thing is weird, though," I insisted.

"It isn't unheard of that a person suffering a medical emergency will cause damage to themselves or their surroundings in an attempt to attract attention. She may have slipped into a sort of trance or epileptic seizure that caused her to do all that damage." I looked at him like he had just started to speak in clicks and buzzes. "Have you talked to Jake?"

"Yeah. I gave him the four, one, one when you guys arrived."

"Did he tell you about Tom?" Blake asked. I shook my head no.

"Cath, I'm sorry, but Tom's condition has worsened." Blake put his hand on my shoulder.

"How can that be? You guys said he came out of surgery fine. That he just needed some time to rest, and he'd be on the road to recovery."

I stared into Blake's face. His blue eyes looked pained, and when he looked at me, he wasn't just talking to me. He was studying my face and my hair and my neck. Why? Why would he look at me with that kind of longing when my boyfriend was sick in the hospital?

"There was some kind of complication. A million and one chance that things could take a turn for the worse. Yet they did," he said softly.

"Well, can I go see him?" I didn't realize I'd clutched Blake's arm. He gently covered my hand with his.

"Cath, he's in a coma."

My knees went weak. This wasn't supposed to happen. A coma? My breath came out in one long, tired sigh.

"What am I supposed to do now, Blake?" I asked him quietly.

"I don't know. But whatever you decide, I'll help you if I'm able." I wanted to hug him. No. That wasn't entirely true. I wanted him to hug *me*. I wanted to feel his strong arms around me and hear him tell me in his Mr. Spock monotone that everything would be all right. That this was just a setback, and the doctors were taking good care of Tom. He'd be back on his police motorcycle in no time at all. Once he was out of the woods.

"Um, I better make sure the door to the babe couple's house is closed," I stuttered.

"Who?" Blake asked.

I explained to him my nickname for the Lourdeses and why in a nutshell. I didn't feel like talking. My mouth had gone dry, and my stomach knotted up. I started to walk in the direction of the house and was on the porch before I realized Blake had followed me.

I turned around before taking hold of the doorknob and looked up at Blake.

"Can you help me get in to see him? His mother is just...she's like a pit bull."

"I'll do my best for you, Cath," he said. For a second, I thought he was going to lean in to me with a kiss. It was like he started but caught himself and pulled back. But he never looked away from my eyes.

I went up and peeked inside before taking hold of the doorknob. I saw the mirror that Bea had been looking at. I didn't realize it was so oddly placed in the room. But I didn't think anything of it. I shut the door and left with Blake.

❦ 9 ❦

NO ADMITTANCE

"How are you feeling?" I asked Bea once she arrived at the café the next morning. "You must be under the weather if I'm here before you are."

"I'm okay," she said, shaking her head. "I am out of sorts, but I think a little change of scenery and work will do the trick."

"What's the matter, honey?" Aunt Astrid asked.

"She's coming down with a cold," I offered, gently patting Bea on the back.

"I just said I'd feel better in a little while," she snapped. "I'm fine." When she looked up, her gaze was hard, but it softened quickly. "I'm just not myself. Nothing a few hundred CCs of orange juice and some hot tea can't fix. I'm sorry."

"Hey, if you want a change of scenery, maybe you could come with me," I said.

"Where are you going?"

I suddenly realized I hadn't said anything to anyone about Tom's condition. I'd known for hours that his condition had gotten worse, and I hadn't said anything. I went home last night, had something to eat, and fell asleep. Bea wasn't the only one out of sorts.

"Blake told me last night that Tom isn't doing well." I looked to my aunt, whose worried face said it all. "He said he slipped into a coma."

"Oh my gosh," Aunt Astrid gasped. She was organizing her receipts at her favorite table and slowly stood up. "Are you all right, Cath?"

"What can I do?" I shrugged. "I can't change any of this. But I don't know how to say this, Aunt Astrid, except to blurt it out. I think his mother has something to do with it."

My aunt looked at me skeptically.

"I'm not a mother," I said. "I don't know how it feels to have a child and be worried about them all the time. She's got such a backward way of doing things. I can't help but wonder if she's causing more harm than good."

"Cath, you always think the worst of people," Bea

said as she looked at her reflection in the tall coffeepot.

"Yeah. And sometimes I'm right," I replied. "So, I'm hoping you guys will come with me to the hospital when Blake calls and says the coast is clear."

"Blake is going to call you?" Aunt Astrid asked. "He's a good man."

"He is, Aunt Astrid. He really is," I said quietly.

"Of course we'll go with you," she said, smoothing my hair. "But first, let me get my daughter some hot tea."

"Thanks, Mom," Bea said.

BUSINESS WAS SLOW TODAY, AND I WAS GLAD for it. I kept jumping every time the café phone rang. For some reason, we were getting a lot of wrong numbers. It was just one of those days, I guessed. Finally, Bea picked up, and I heard her say hello to Blake. Without looking at me, she called my name and held out the phone.

"Hello?"

"Cath, it's Blake. Can you make it to the hospital?" he asked.

"Yeah. I'm going to bring my aunt and Bea too. Is that okay?"

"I don't think it will hurt," he replied and told me that he'd be waiting in the lobby for us. I looked to my aunt, who stood up from her table.

"We'll close up for a couple hours. It won't hurt business." She winked as she pulled her long maroon sweater from the back of the chair and swung it over her shoulders.

"You ready, Bea?" I asked. She was staring down at a spoon in her hand. "Bea?" I tapped her on the shoulder, making her jump.

"Don't sneak up on me!" she griped.

"Sneak up? It's like working on a submarine behind this counter. Sneak up. What are you, daft?" I grabbed her purse from under the counter and handed it to her.

"I don't know what I'm so jumpy for." Bea shook her head. "Yeah. I'm ready. I'll drive."

"Why are you driving?" I asked.

"Because if you get emotional, calmer heads need to steer the vessel," Bea replied.

"Okay. But remember that the speed limit is our friend. If we do the speed limit, we get where we want to be faster." I looked at my aunt, who was laughing.

Bea didn't reply to my ribbing. In fact, when we got in her car, she spent an awkward couple of minutes adjusting the mirrors, looking at her reflection, then fixing the mirror again until finally she was happy with where they were situated.

I thought it was odd, but when I looked at my aunt in the passenger seat, she didn't seem to be affected by it. So, I just shrugged it off. Who was I to accuse anyone of acting strange?

When we finally made it to the hospital, after hitting every red light along the way, I was sure I'd see flyers of my face taken from security footage in a red circle with a red slash across it and the words NO ADMITTANCE written in big bold letters. But all I saw as we piled into the slowly self-rotating door was Blake standing at the information desk, his hands in the pockets of his trousers.

He walked up to us, looking serious. "Jake is waiting on the third floor," he said as he slipped his fingers around my arm. "Mrs. Warner is not there. She has left the property. I've got an officer downstairs keeping an eye out for her. They'll let me know if she shows up on the premises while you're still visiting. Remember, we'll need to move when she returns because what we are doing isn't exactly on the right side of the law."

"Blake, you and Jake won't get in trouble, will you?" I took hold of his fingers on my arm and squeezed.

"We've been in trouble for worse," he replied, and I saw the right corner of his mouth curl slightly.

As much as I wanted to be grateful to Blake and Jake, I was feeling guilty for being more concerned about them than I was for Tom. I didn't want Tom to suffer. He was so wonderful. He didn't deserve this to happen to him. But it was like it was happening to the friend of a friend that I didn't have a connection with. Every day I didn't see Tom was another day I grew further from him. I heard my own thoughts saying *it wasn't him, it was me*. How cliché.

As we rode the elevator, I barely saw anyone around me. My aunt talked with Blake. She always did. It was obvious that she had a soft spot in her heart for him. I was not sure why she continued to treat him like a long-lost nephew. But at the moment, I was glad she was talking, taking the spotlight off me.

When the elevator doors opened, we saw Jake. I hurried ahead of Blake toward the door Jake was standing in front of. It was the same room I had seen Patience and the faceless man in front of. The blinds were closed to the hallway.

"Hey, Cath. Take your time," Jake said. I nodded and went inside the room.

Jake didn't close the door behind me, but I got the feeling I was isolated in there. I looked over my shoulder, and the door was wide open. But every time I looked away, it was like the door was shut. Carefully, I tiptoed toward the bed. A curtain was pulled partially up, preventing me from seeing his face. As I peeked around the hanging sheet, I was shocked to see him just sleeping.

His eyes were closed. His wavy dark hair was mussed. His hands were at his sides, with IVs attached to one of his arms. There wasn't anything out of the ordinary except for the horrible white snake that was down his throat, helping him to breathe.

"Tom?" I said, half expecting him to open his eyes. He didn't. I walked up and gently took his hand in both of mine. "Oh, Tom. I don't know if you can hear me. You've got to get better."

I swallowed hard and looked around the room. It was dreary and sad with no flowers or cards. That was hard for me to believe because he was a cop, and they all stuck together, and if one of their own were in the hospital, they'd be visiting around the clock.

There should have been balloons and get-well banners.

"This isn't normal. You were getting better after your surgery. Jake and Blake both told me you were. Tom…" I suddenly felt very tired. My eyes filled with tears. "Tom, I don't know what I'm feeling anymore. I'm pulling for you. But you've got to get out of this so you can find the right person to take care of you. It isn't me. This isn't the right time. I know. But when is it ever the right time?" I wiped my nose with the back of my hand.

The darkness was overwhelming. I walked over to the window and threw the curtains open. The bright-blue sky smiled in and made the machines and the wires that were hooked up to Tom look more helpful than intimidating.

I walked back over to the bed and brushed his hair across his forehead. He was so handsome, with his five o'clock shadow and chiseled jawline. What was I thinking, not being attracted to him anymore? What was wrong with me? He accepted me. He didn't think I was weird or scary. We were like kindred spirits since he said himself that he had some strange experiences in his life. Why was I throwing this gift away? Why was I determined to do it now, when he was completely unaware of me? Was I really that much of a coward?

"All right, Tom." I sniffed. "You want to just lie there. I can't do anything about it. But unless you want to talk to me so we can handle our situation like adults, there is nothing more I can do for you." I rubbed my arms. It felt as if the air conditioning had kicked on.

Again, I was getting the feeling that the room was closing in on me. Like I was trapped in a box that was getting smaller and the air was getting thinner.

"Tom. Can you squeeze my hand?" I slipped my fingers beneath his and folded his hand over mine. "I'm making it as easy as possible. Just a tiny squeeze if you can hear me."

I waited.

"I know you're in there. Just a little squeeze? I'll get Bea to help you. You know she's really good at finding out what's blocking someone from getting better. Can you just let me know you're there? One squeeze? Don't be a jerk, Tom," I whined with tears in my eyes. "You're doing this just to make me upset, aren't you? It's payback for all the sarcastic remarks I've made. Fine. Next time, I'll be the one in the coma, and you can see what it feels like."

Nothing except the creepy sound of him breathing with the help of a machine.

"You can't stay like this, Tom. You can't." I squeezed his hand.

It was deathly quiet.

But then there was a screech from the hallway. The howl of a wild woman shook the entire floor, and that was when I felt it. Tom squeezed my hand so tightly I thought he was going to break my fingers. He let me go only when I saw his mother standing in the doorway.

🌿 10 🪶

BATTLEFIELD

"What are you doing here?" Patience all but screamed.

"I came to see Tom," I stuttered. She was still in the same clothes she had been wearing before. "I...he...just squeezed..."

"Get out! Get out of this room! You've killed him. Do you understand me? You've killed him!"

I just stood there, staring. First, I was in shock that she was screaming so loudly at me in a public place. Half a dozen nurses came running and warned us both that security was on its way.

"I'm his mother," she hissed at the nurses. "That witch has no right to be here! She's making my son sick!"

"No, I'm not." I started to cry.

That was when I saw Blake pushing his way past the nurses. He grabbed my arm and pulled me out of the room, where Bea and Aunt Astrid were standing, dumbstruck.

"Bea, you've got to help him," I begged. "There's something else in there. You have to help him."

She looked at me like she wasn't sure what I was talking about. Then her eyes snapped open like she'd remembered she had this unique gift that could possibly save Tom's life. Before she could enter the room, the nurses stopped her.

"You're going to have to leave," one nurse said as if she were giving orders on a battlefield. She looked like someone who had been forced to do this before. There was no anger in her eyes. Just a seriousness that meant she wasn't going to lose her job over people like us.

"There's something else in there," I whispered to my aunt, who put her arm around me. "Whatever it is, it's going to kill him. Or worse. Keep him trapped like this forever."

"You get out of here!" Patience screamed again as the nurses warned her to stop making such a scene or she would be the one to leave. Daggers came from her eyes as she glared at each one of them. But her hateful look stopped on me.

"You did this. You stay away from Tom. She'll kill my boy if she comes anywhere near him. She'll kill him. I know it."

"You'll stop that talk this instant," Aunt Astrid said, making Patience step back nervously. It seemed that my wobbly aunt was the only one who put any fear into Patience. I wondered why.

It was obvious since my aunt first met Patience that she knew something was wrong with her. She banned her from ever coming into the café because Patience did this same thing, only not so loudly.

"When Tom is better, we'll be back. Not for you. But for Tom. And if you want to test your ability to stop us, to stop me, well, you go right ahead," Aunt Astrid said, making Patience shrink.

"You keep them out of my son's room," Patience sneered before closing his door. It clicked with a finality that made me feel a lump in my throat.

Was this going to be the last time I saw Tom? What was I supposed to do now? I didn't care for him the way I used to. It wasn't because of anything he did or didn't do. We just drifted apart. Okay, maybe I drifted. I was going to tell him before this happened. But now, what kind of a selfish woman would I look like to drop him when he was in a coma? My gosh, it sounded like the script to a bad daytime soap opera.

Blake, Jake, Aunt Astrid, Bea, and I piled into the elevator and headed to the first floor.

"What the heck happened?" I looked at Blake. "You said you were going to come get me if you got word Patience was back."

"I don't know what happened." The look on his face was as if he suddenly realized he didn't have his wallet.

"Bea? Where were you? I needed you in there! Something is happening to Tom, and he's going to die if we don't help. You were the only person who could have given us some kind of lead. What happened?" I was trembling with anger.

My family had never let me down before. But as I looked at Bea, she wouldn't even look at me. She just stared into the reflection in the elevator doors.

"Calm down, honey." Aunt Astrid tried to soothe me, but I was having none of it. I felt sick and disgusted and humiliated. Patience was obviously crazy, but even worse, she was violent too. Maybe she wouldn't have come at me, swinging, but she was definitely out to verbally tear me to shreds. At the moment, I felt like that was worse.

"I don't want to calm down!" I said as the doors

slid open on the first floor. The sight of all the other visitors and doctors and administrators made me mad. They were going about their business and didn't know what had just happened. I wanted to be like them. I wanted to be oblivious to the paranormal and the occult. I hated that my family came from this because, even with all our gifts, we weren't helping anyone. "Tom squeezed my hand! He's alert in there! But as soon as his mother stepped in the room, he stopped. You could have helped, Bea."

I didn't realize I was shouting until I took a breath and saw the entire lobby looking at me. I was sure I wasn't the only person to ever have an emotional outburst in a hospital. So, I did what I figured any normal person would do. I stormed out.

"Wait!" I heard Blake behind me. "Cath, wait!"

I stopped, and something came over me. I don't know what it was, but I looked Blake straight in the eyes. "You said you were going to get me out of there before Patience could see me." My eyes filled with tears. "How did she get past you? You're supposed to be a detective. Don't you slink around unnoticed all the time?"

"I'm so sorry, Cath. Something caught my attention. I went to investigate. By the time I got back, the fireworks had already started. There was no excuse for it."

He stood with that stoic look on his face. I was so angry I wanted to slap him, but I didn't. That would have just made me feel worse.

"I want to be alone."

"Cath, I saw something in there. You're the only person I know who might have an idea what it was."

"Are you kidding? You drop the ball on something as simple as letting me know the dragon queen is approaching, and now you want my help? That sounds, well, stupid." Not my greatest retort, but under the circumstances, it was the best I could do.

"There was a man there, and I swear, he had no face."

❧ II ❧

FACIAL DEFORMITY

I looked at Blake and waited. Was this a trap? Was he trying to bait me to see how I would react and then decide that I was crazy?

"He was wearing a black suit. He had on a hat. He looked strangely out of place, but no one seemed to notice him but me. I stepped away to follow him and see who he was going to visit. Perhaps it was just a facial deformity or maybe a trick of the light. But then he looked right at me."

"Why are you telling me this? Didn't you see what happened in there? Didn't you hear what Patience said?" My vision blurred. I don't know why I started crying.

"That's why I'm telling you this. I don't know if you are a witch or not, Cath. All I know is that strange things happen when you are around. Some scary. Some beautiful. But you are the only person I can talk to about it because you know so much more than I do."

I stopped crying. My breath hitched in my throat, and I calmed down. Of course I had to wipe my nose and only had the hem of my shirt. Like the true lady that I was, I used the back of my hand. Blake stepped closer and handed me a kerchief.

"Thanks." I took the hankie and blew my nose. "I'm sorry, but I think I must have caught some kind of virus in the hospital because I just hallucinated. I thought you said I know more than you." I chuckled as I held the hankie in front of my mouth and nose.

"Tell me what that man was. He was real. He was standing there. It wasn't a trick of the light. And I wasn't hallucinating any more than you are right now." He took a step toward me.

With renewed attitude, I told him what Bea had said to me.

"So, they are messengers?" Blake asked.

"I don't know for sure. But she said it is common to see them at hospitals."

He scratched his chin. His expression was stoic. It had to be a rare feeling for him to digest something so abstract. He was so comfortable in the world of facts that I think this actually caused his brain to freeze, like drinking a lime slushy too fast, something I'm prone to do on hot summer days.

"Well, I appreciate you explaining that to me. I'm sorry that Patience Warner made such a scene. You didn't deserve that just for loving her son." His tone was angry, but his words were controlled.

I wanted to tell Blake I didn't love Tom. It was the first time I wanted to even admit it, let alone say it out loud. But I didn't. It would have been too much with all that had happened.

"I better get back to the café. I need to talk to my aunt and Bea." I shoved my hands in my back pockets.

"I'm happy to drive you. We just need to get Jake." He offered.

"I think I'd like to take the bus. I feel like being alone, if you don't mind."

Blake was nicer to me than he'd ever been. I was sure it wouldn't last. He'd be back to his condescending self soon enough. He was always so funny when he tried to rationalize certain things, especially when they had to do with emotions. Like the feeling people got around Christmas or when they saw a shooting star at night. It was almost like he said that stuff just to be funny but didn't know it.

Trying to focus while on the bus was like skipping a stone across the water. My mind would touch on the surface, but whatever it picked up didn't stay, as just as quickly, it was off to touch on something else until it just sank.

"What are you doing, Cath? Your boyfriend is in a coma," I muttered.

Just as I stepped off the bus a block from the café, I saw Bea leaving. Where was she going? It was not closing time. Maybe she was really getting sick. As much as I wanted to run to her and see if she was okay, I couldn't help but feel a little angry at her, so I let her go off alone. That in itself was bothersome. Bea and I were always so close. I never thought for a second that she didn't have my back. But something was tilting our footing, and we just didn't seem in sync. I was just going to add that to the long list of grievances I had about my life at the moment.

When I stepped into the café, my aunt rushed to me, wrapping me in her arms. I hugged her back.

"Cath, I am so sorry." She smoothed my hair.

"It's okay. What is that old saying? If you want to make God laugh, make plans?" I chuckled.

"Yes, that is true. But I think that our problem was that we made a plan like we were just dealing with a hostile woman. I should have known. I should have protected all of us before we went in there. What was I thinking? That's the problem." She slapped her forehead. "I wasn't thinking."

"Aunt Astrid, Bea could have helped. What's the matter with her?"

"I think she and Jake are having problems. Whenever an empath is struggling with their own feelings, then you can bet their empathic ability to help others is severely retarded. She just needs some time. They'll work things out."

"So, what do we do in the meantime?"

"I'm afraid we'll have to wait. There was something else going on in that hospital. Something our friend Patience Warner has her hand in." My aunt headed toward the bunker.

The bunker was the Greenstone witches' clubhouse. There was a small door off the kitchen that led to a tiny basement. It was furnished with cozy secondhand chairs and side tables. Bea had decorated it a little to make it homier. Aunt Astrid had some of her spell books in there. I supplied the hot plate, Twinkies, and potato chips.

"Flip that sign to closed, and follow me," she said.

Just as I snapped the lock in place, our phone rang. Fearing it was something bad about Tom's condition, I leaned over the counter and snatched the phone up. It was Jake.

"Hey, Cath. Is Bea there?"

"No. Aunt Astrid sent her home because she wasn't feeling well. Anything I can do for you?" I heard him let out a big sigh.

"Well, I thought you might like to know that we got the autopsy report back from the coroner on Mrs. Kitt. Her heart exploded and then..."

"So, she had a heart attack?" I nodded.

"No. Her heart exploded. Then it turned to stone. It was like someone hooked it up to the battery of a nuclear sub and threw the switch. Then made a concrete replica of the pieces," he said. "They are running a few more tests, but the guys in the cooler say they've never seen anything like it."

"I'll bet." I looked at my aunt. "Thanks for calling, Jake. You might want to try Bea at home. Although she might be resting if she's under the weather."

"Yeah. Okay." He sounded heartbroken. "And, Cath, I'm sorry about what happened at the hospital. I was trying to talk to Bea, and things just went from bad to worse."

"Don't worry about it, Jake. You'll suffer my wrath on another day," I joked.

"I don't doubt it."

When I hung up and told my aunt what Jake said about Mrs. Kitt, her face grew pale.

"What's the matter?"

"Hit the lights. We've got some research to do. And I'm afraid we don't have a lot of time."

🦎 12 🦎

REARRANGED

Aunt Astrid and I spent the remaining few hours in the bunker searching through her spell books and paranormal creature reference books, but I still had no real idea what we were looking for.

"There are only a couple of things that can cause the human heart to explode, and even fewer that will turn it to stone. But I can't focus. I can't recall what it is I'm trying to find." She tapped the side of her head with a clenched fist.

"Maybe you have what Bea has. Maybe there is a bug going around. The flu will do that to you. You can't concentrate, and you're tired without even realizing it. Yes, the flu. That's probably what's got you guys."

"Maybe you are right." She didn't really look convinced. "I'm afraid we better call it a day. Do me a favor. Go home and stay there. Have some soup, get some rest, and let's meet here in the morning like nothing is out of the ordinary."

"Okay." I wasn't really certain this was the path to take. Especially when she just said we didn't have a lot of time.

"Promise?"

"I promise, Aunt Astrid. Straight home and here again at oh-seven-hundred hours."

She stayed behind and locked the place up as I walked to my house. As I was getting closer, I could have sworn I saw Bea's head of red hair crossing the street from the babe couple's house to her house.

Since my cousin was claiming to be out of sorts, I decided to just stage a stakeout. I would watch her house throughout the night and see if there was any movement. I was ashamed to admit my stakeout skills were sorely lacking. I got hungry within ten minutes of surveillance and stepped away to make a bologna sandwich.

When I came back, I realized I'd forgotten a glass of Coke. Then after about an hour of watching, I fell asleep. When I woke up on the couch, it was four hours later, and Treacle was meowing at the kitchen window.

"Hey, have you seen anything weird around the neighborhood today?" I asked him.

"Funny you should ask. Peanut Butter is having some issues."

"Peanut Butter? What's wrong with him?" I was instantly worried.

"He says his mom is sick."

"Sick with the flu or sick…?" I made circles with my index finger at the side of my head.

"A little of both. But you know Peanut Butter. He has the tendency to exaggerate, still being so young. Just an inch above being a kitten. But he did say that she keeps peeking out the window."

"You're kidding!" I clapped. "I'll bet she was watching me watch her and didn't make a move. Of course, I really don't know because I fell asleep, but I wouldn't be surprised."

"What?"

"Never mind. I'm just talking out loud. Now, because of that catnap, I'm wide-awake. And my laundry is all done, and so are the dishes."

"Well, I've had a busy day." Treacle stretched and yawned and purred as he climbed up onto my lap. *"Time to go to sleep."*

"I'm going out."

"Uh-oh. You know what happened the last time you went out in the middle of the night."

"I'm going to see Old Murray," I said. "I'm staying away from the hospital all together."

Old Murray Willis was dedicated to the animals in his care. It wasn't uncommon for him to be there long after closing hours tending to the strays, talking to them, giving them the love and attention they needed and deserved.

The Wonder Falls Animal Shelter was only fifteen minutes from my house. When I arrived, I wasn't surprised to see Old Murray's truck. But the familiar plain sedan was a shock. That was Blake Samberg's sedan.

When I knocked on the glass door, I could see they were both surprised to see me. I waved and smiled as Old Murray shuffled to the door.

"Girl, what in the world are you doing out at this hour?"

"It's too early to go to sleep but too late to go to work. So, I thought I'd pay you a visit and see if you needed anything." I had to look up a couple inches to see into Old Murray's kind face. He always wore a plaid shirt, and his hands were big, calloused, and as gentle as lambs.

"I've got my partner here helping out. You know Detective Samberg."

"Of course I do." I waved. "Hi, Blake."

"Cath." He looked at me suspiciously.

"Murray, how are those cats you took from my neighbors' house? Are they doing all right?" I asked innocently.

"They're doing fine. We haven't had any luck contacting the owners. But if they are travelling through Europe, as I've been told, then it might be best to just wait until they return. The cats can stay here. We've got plenty of room and plenty of help. They can play and stretch out as long as need be."

"Are they with the other cats?"

"You know the way, Cath. Go on and say hi."

I did know the way, as I'd volunteered at Old Murray's on a regular basis. I walked down the hallway and to the room with the cat silhouette on the door. Once inside, I was happy to see that there were just two cats sharing one cage, snuggled up against one another, purring happily. The other empty cages meant everyone had found a good home.

"Hello? Are you guys sleeping?"

Two lazy heads lifted and looked at me. One cat

was an adorable tuxedo cat, white with black spots. The other was a tabby. Black, white, and orange.

"Who are you? You aren't our people."

"No. Your people are still travelling. I'm the person who got Old Murray to come and get you out of the house."

Slowly they unwound themselves from each other and sniffed at me.

"Thank you so much. The woman didn't feed us. She didn't change our litter box."

"That's what I wanted to ask you about. Was she mean to you?"

"I'll tell her what happened."

The tabby purred. *"No, I'll tell her."*

"You take forever to tell a story."

"But I know what happened," the tabby replied.

"The woman had a problem with the mirrors," the tuxedo cat purred.

"The mirrors?" I wrinkled my face.

"She stared into them for hours," the tabby added.

"Yes, hours."

"Do you know why?" I asked.

"No," the tabby said. *"She didn't do it before the house was rearranged."*

"What do you mean rearranged?" I leaned closer so I wasn't talking too loudly.

"After our people left us," Tabby purred.

"Yes, they just left us," Tuxedo pouted.

"No. They're coming back. I promise. But what do you mean the house was rearranged?"

"The lady let in some people who cleaned and painted and rearranged everything in the house," Tabby continued.

"That's weird," I muttered.

I didn't remember seeing any trucks in their driveway, but then again, I didn't really pay any attention to their house. Maybe Bea saw something.

"We didn't like how they rearranged things. It was clumsy and hard for us to chase each other around like we used to," Tuxedo said.

"Did they do anything else? Anything that you thought was weird?" It was a long shot. Anyone who ever owned a cat knew that their definition of weird and ours was quite different. They thought it was perfectly normal to climb out on the ledge of a twenty-story building to take a look around.

"They just made the mirrors easier for the lady to stare into," Tabby replied.

"The lady stared in the mirrors constantly," Tuxedo added.

"Did she say anything?"

"She just said how beautiful. At first, we thought she was talking about us," Tuxedo said, nudging his head

against Tabby's. *"But we were wrong. She stopped caring about us."*

Just then the door to the room swung open, and Blake walked in.

"Who are you talking to?" he asked.

❧ 13 ❧

INTERNAL PETRIFICATION OF ORGANS

Blake quietly walked up to me and stuck his finger tenderly into the cage to stroke the tabby.

Tabby and Tuxedo began to meow, meow, meow.

"*Me.*"

"*She was talking to me.*"

"*No, it's obvious she was talking to me.*"

"*It was me.*"

"*You wish. It was me.*"

"You know me," I said. "I talk to animals like they are people. You've seen me with Treacle. You'd think I was discussing philosophy with Aristotle the way I talk things out with him." I chuckled. I looked at the cats.

"He doesn't know I can talk to you," I said in my head.

"We won't tell him," Tabby said.

"Hey, mister! We know all about you!" Tuxedo shouted in a loud meow then started laughing.

"Yeah, we know everything!" Tabby joined in, making me click my tongue and roll my eyes at the two pranksters.

"Your people will be home to get you soon. But in the meantime, Old Murray will take good care of you. I'll come check on you in a few days."

The cats seemed in excellent spirits and looked quite healthy. I headed toward the door. Blake followed me.

"Where are you going now?" he asked.

"I guess I'll go back home. I couldn't sleep, but now I'm getting tired." I smiled up at Blake, who didn't smile back. "I forgot you volunteered here. It's a nice place to be. I always did my best thinking when I was here. I don't usually have good ideas. Maybe I should volunteer more often and I won't get myself into pickles like I did today."

"That wasn't your fault," he said.

"I'm afraid if I admit that to myself, I'll sound like a martyr. I tried to get Patience to like me, but she already had ideas of the kind of girl Tom should take seriously. There was no way I was going to fit that mold." I put my hands on my hips. "It's for the best."

"You shouldn't let her discourage you. If it's what you want, you should fight for it." He looked at the two cats, who were too busy grooming one another to pay any attention to us.

"See, there's the problem. I'm not sure it is what I want." The words just fell out of my mouth like someone deposited a penny in a gumball machine. I didn't look at Blake, but out of the corner of my eye, I saw his head snap in my direction. My cheeks flared up.

Blake put his hands in his pockets. "So, you want to tell me what you are doing out here at this time of night?"

"It has to do with Mrs. Kitt."

"Well, I think I can put your mind at ease. The cases of internal petrification of organs are rare. Almost seven trillion to one. But they are not impossible. From the quick research I've done and what the coroner has said, this transformation could have been taking place inside Mrs. Kitt for years."

"Internal petrification of organs?" That was a gross concept.

"Like a geode sometimes cracks under pressure,

so was the situation with her heart. Let's face it, she wasn't in the best health, and she was older."

"She told us she was exercising and eating better," I said.

"It might have been a little too late. And the sudden change in diet and physical activity might have been just the ticket to push her over the limit."

"All the more reason for me not to exercise." I nodded. He didn't smile. That was the Blake I'd learned to know and love. Wait, I didn't mean the love part. Or did I? "Did she have any contact with anyone before she died? Is there any next of kin to be notified?"

Blake shook his head. So, after all this, I'd hit a brick wall. Petrified organs? Exploding innards?

"Hey." He finally spoke, and I was glad he did. If the awkward silence had gone on much longer, I would have had to tell a joke, and I was terrible at telling jokes. They came out all wrong and sounded more like tragedies. "What are you doing after you leave here?"

"I was just going to go back home. Try and stay out of trouble. Why?"

"I'll follow you."

"It's okay, Blake. I can get home safely."

"I'm not worried about that." He looked at his

watch. There. See? It only took a second for him to go from sweet to sour. "How would you like to check out Mrs. Kitt's house with me? I've got the feeling we might have overlooked something."

"Heck yeah," I said, not even trying to hide my excitement. "Count me in."

After we said goodbye to Old Murray and drove separately to my place, I wondered if Bea was still watching the house. If she was, I had no doubt I'd be hearing all the ohs and ahs about what a cute couple Blake and I made and how great we were together.

As we walked across the grass to Mrs. Kitt's house, which still had police tape on the door, I looked at my cousin's house. There was a light on in the bedroom and one on the first floor. I thought it was a little strange at this hour, but maybe I wasn't the only one who couldn't sleep.

"What do you think we should look for?" I asked as Blake pulled the tape aside and opened the door.

"I'm not sure. Like I said, Mrs. Kitt's condition is rare but has happened. But something in my gut says there is something more to this story." He sighed.

"Never ignore your gut," I whispered.

He looked down and smirked, his right eyebrow going up á la Mr. Spock. I shrugged and stepped inside. Blake pulled his flashlight out and shined the bright beam toward the bathroom where I found Mrs. Kitt. Just past it was the kitchen.

Blake stood at the threshold of the bathroom. He was reflected a hundred times in the cracked spiderweb that was the mirror. Blake looked at the ground and seemed to be studying the chalked-out area where Mrs. Kitt's body had been.

I got a bit of the heebie-jeebies, so I inched my way toward the kitchen. A back-porch light illuminated the fridge, the stove, the counter, and the kitchen table. As I looked around, the place looked depressingly normal. On the fridge was a calendar that had a doctor's appointment scheduled, a trip to the hair salon, dry cleaning to pick up, and a visit from a person called Shesha.

"Shesha?" I muttered. "Shesha a real piece of work. Shesha shashy gal from Sharatoga."

"What are you saying?" Blake asked.

"Nothing. I'm just talking to myself to keep the spookies away."

As I looked over the fridge, I saw a business card that was stuck beneath a magnet with cooking measurements on it. When I pulled it out, I was surprised to see the name Shesha repeated on it. The business was called Nine Lemons in a Bowl. She touted better living through feng shui.

I wondered if the woman on this business card was the person the cats said rearranged the babe couple's house. It certainly couldn't hurt to give it a try. But I had to keep this to myself. If I told Blake that the babe couple's cats told me about the people rearranging furniture, I was sure he'd have a long talk with Aunt Astrid to have me committed.

Before he could take notice, I pocketed the business card and tiptoed back to the bathroom where he was still standing.

"Her death can be explained by science. But what is it with the mirrors that I can't shake?" Blake asked, squinting at his reflection.

"Mirrors?"

"Every mirror in the house looks like this one. They've all been shattered, and I can't figure out why." He rubbed his chin. "We determined there was no one else in the house at her time of death. There was no forced entry. No furniture disrupted or any other signs of a struggle. She was alone when she died."

"She came into the café before she was found," I said. "I'm sure Bea told Jake."

Blake turned to me like he'd forgotten I was there.

"Jake didn't say anything."

"Oh. Well." I repeated the story to Blake, telling him how nasty Mrs. Kitt was to Bea and Aunt Astrid. "She didn't bother with me too much." I cleared my throat. "She knew she'd have gotten her clock cleaned." I tugged at my collar.

"You said she was a nice old lady who never bothered anyone." Blake didn't catch my attempt at humor. I wasn't surprised.

"She was until she started working out and wearing her hoochie outfits. I'm not sure what it was all about. All I could come up with was some kind of midlife crisis. Aunt Astrid said she was a widow for some time, and maybe loneliness had gotten the best of her." I shrugged. "But what she said had Bea very upset. I'm surprised she didn't tell Jake about it. He's that kind of knight in shining armor made for instances like that. You know, swoop in with a dozen roses and reservations at a fancy restaurant to make Bea feel better."

I watched Blake's face in the light of the flashlight as he digested everything I'd told him.

"Maybe that's it. Maybe she just had a psychotic episode and smashed all the mirrors." He shrugged. "It doesn't sound right, but it might be all we've got."

"I've learned that when I hit a brick wall or feel

I've exhausted my options, it's best to sleep on it. Everything looks different in the sunlight."

"Did your aunt Astrid tell you that?" He smirked.

"No. Well, she might have said something like that but not exactly. I perfected it from whoever said it first."

Looking around the dark house as Blake continued to ponder the broken mirror, I took a few steps into the living room. There was a mirror on the wall, and it was smashed. I hadn't noticed before.

"What did she use to break the mirrors?" I called out to Blake. There was no answer. "Blake?"

✾ 14 ✾

PLAYING DETECTIVE

ear caught me, and I stood still, holding my breath. I didn't have a light or a gun or anything. I'd followed him into the house of a dead person, knowing full well that there might be a supernatural woogie-boogie in the place. What was I thinking?

"Blake, you better answer me!" I hissed into the darkness. I wanted him to hear me but, at the same time, didn't want to give away my position if there were any demons or creatures roaming the empty house. It was a fine line to walk.

"What?" He leaned around the corner with the flashlight underneath his chin. I yelped and jumped three feet in the air, like Treacle would when something spooked him.

"Not funny, nerd." I stomped over to him. "I said, what did Mrs. Kitt use to break the mirrors? Did she use her hands? I don't see anything left on the ground, and I didn't see anything when I found her in the bathroom."

"That's a good question. I don't think any of us thought about that," Blake said. "Can I use your phone?"

"Sure, it's at my house. I don't carry my cell phone. No one's ever trying to call me," I said, making my way toward the door.

We stepped outside, and Blake put the tape back up around the door. We cut through the grass and went inside my house, where Blake got a warm greeting from Treacle, who had been sleeping on my bed.

I handed Blake my phone and went into the kitchen to grab a couple of Cokes.

"Lou. It's Samberg. On Kitt's body. Were there any contusions on the hands, knuckles, palms? Actually, were there any cuts or scratches that would be the result of smashing a mirror?"

This was cool. Now I'd have the coroner's number on my cell. That could be interesting if I ever felt courageous enough to call and find out about someone in the cooler. The thought made me shake my head at myself.

"Nothing? Nothing out of the ordinary? Well, other than the petrified insides. Yes. Okay. Thanks a lot, Lou. Sorry to bother you so late."

That was the end of the call, and Blake came into the kitchen, his brow wrinkled in deep thought. He handed me my phone and pulled out a seat at the table.

"Coke?"

"Yeah." He nodded as he sat down. "So, there was nothing on the body to indicate Mrs. Kitt used her hands or body to smash the glass. We must have missed something."

I shrugged. I had no idea what to tell him, and my energy level was quickly depleting. I was getting more tired by the minute. But at the same time, I didn't want Blake to leave. It was nice having him here. But I yawned and ruined everything.

"Gosh, Cath. I completely forgot about the time." He looked at his watch. "You've got to be at the café tomorrow, and Jake will be expecting me to pick him up."

"I'm sorry. I was only yawning due to a temporary lack of oxygen. I read that somewhere."

"It's true, but it also indicates when a body is

tired. I think we better end our investigation for tonight." He didn't smile but nodded as if to reinforce the fact it was late and I was tired.

"Can you keep me posted as to what you find out about how the mirrors got smashed? That's a real mystery. I'd like to know." I took a sip of the Coke. The cold sugary drink tasted great.

"Of course." He stood up and walked to the door. I trailed behind him. Treacle gave a pleasant meow from the couch, stretching his left paw straight out, splaying his toes but quickly tucking it back beneath his belly.

As I held the door open and Blake stepped onto the porch, he turned around, with his hands in his pockets and his eyes on his feet.

"Thank you for coming with me."

"Sure. I mean, it's right next door. What could I say? Sorry, that's a little too far out of my way?" I was babbling.

"I wouldn't suggest going over there again. I'm going to talk to Jake, and we're going to have to do a more thorough scrub-down of the place. We need to find the object used to break the mirrors, and that may provide a more solid lead. We better not contaminate the scene any more than we already have." He didn't grin or smirk.

I nodded and crossed my heart. "Promise."

"Good night, Cath."

"Night, Blake." I closed the door, flipped the dead bolt, and leaned against it. "You weren't a very welcoming host," I teased Treacle.

"He wasn't here long enough. I would have poured on the charm if he'd have stayed. I like Blake."

I nodded and headed back to the kitchen.

"Did you hear what I said?" he called after me.

"What?"

"I said I like Blake."

"Okay." I smirked. "What do you want? A medal?"

"You are supposed to say you do too."

"Is that so?"

"Yes. It's written all over your face. You just needed Tom to show you the way."

"Oh gosh. I forgot all about Tom." I smacked my head. "Did the phone ring while I was gone? I hope nothing bad has happened to him. I mean, anything worse than what he's already going through."

What kind of person was I? My boyfriend was in a coma after getting shot at work, and I was off with Blake, playing detective.

"I'm a horrible person." I sighed to Treacle, who hopped off the couch and circled my legs.

"No, you're not. You're my person, and I know you better than anyone else. Your heart is too big for Tom. He can't hold it. As much as I like him, he just doesn't have the stuff."

Treacle sat down like a beautiful, sleek black statue and looked up at me. I scooped him up in my arms. He was soft and gave me a good headbutt to the chin while his internal motor continued to run.

"I don't know, Treacle. I feel like a monster. He could really be in trouble and..."

Before I could finish my thought, there was a pounding on my front door. I thought it was Blake and something was wrong. Quickly, I set Treacle on the table and dashed to the door. On tiptoes, I peeked through the peephole and was surprised to see Bea there.

"What's the matter?" I asked as I opened the door. Then I gasped. "What are you wearing?"

My normally stylish yet conservative cousin was standing on my stoop, wearing a tank top and skintight jeans that I'd never seen her wear before. I was the jean wearer in the family, and they were never so tight they looked like they might be cutting off circulation.

"What was Blake doing here?" she snapped.

"He wanted to check out Mrs. Kitt's place one

more time and asked if I wanted to go with him. Why?"

"Do you really think he's interested in you? Don't kid yourself, Cath. You've got a long way to go before you could get the attention of a guy like that."

She looked at me in a way that was all too familiar. Again, I was bombarded with visions of Darla Castellano.

My high school nemesis, Darla Castellano, made my primary teenage years a living hell. She was beautiful and popular and seemed to have everything going for her. I, on the other hand, was plain and awkward and liked to just keep to my small group of friends.

It was always a mystery why she chose to pick on me. Even now when I saw her in town, those feelings of anger would just bubble up, and my aunt would have to put a binding spell on me to prevent me from giving her a scorching case of scabies or maybe uncontrollable dandruff.

But even though I never really did anything to her, Darla still glared at me like I was a boil on the face of humanity. It was the same look I was getting from my cousin at this very moment.

"What are you talking about, Bea?" She'd never spoken to me like that. We grew up together. Her flaming-red hair and cute figure still turned heads as we walked down the street. But I was never jealous of her. We were different, but our name was still Greenstone, and that made us strong together.

"Look, it's about time you know that he's not interested in you. He's just using you to be closer to me." Bea shifted from one leg to the other and folded her arms over her chest.

"Bea, what are you talking about?"

"I just thought it was about time you know. You've been such a burden on everyone for so long. Everybody is tired of carrying your weight. Maybe if you did something with yourself, you could get a man."

"You mean a man like Jake, your husband, who is coming across the street right now?"

I looked at Jake, who was in baggy flannel pajama bottoms and a matching top. The neighbors were going to start wondering why so many people were coming to my place in their pajamas. Any way I looked at it, it wasn't good.

"Bea!" he called.

I looked at Bea's face, and she looked disgusted, as if Jake were the worst person who she could possibly run into right now.

"I just thought you should know," she whispered

to me before turning around and trying to stomp right past Jake.

"Bea, what are you doing out here? Why are you dressed like that?"

"Get out of my way," she said, holding her hands up as if Jake were covered with sludge.

"Bea, come home."

"Don't touch me, or I swear I'll scream and get the cops here." She yanked her hand away from Jake and glared at him.

Jake looked like he'd just seen his dog get run over by a Mack truck. He stood in my driveway as Bea quickly hustled back to their house, slamming the door with such force it made my front window rattle.

"Jake? What is that all about?" I stepped outside and went up to him.

"I don't know, Cath. She's not the same person. I don't know what's wrong with her, but she hasn't been at home for hours. She came in for a minute and then left to come over here. Did she say anything to you?"

I told him what Bea had said, and I thought he was about to cry.

"I don't think there is any truth to that," I soothed, rubbing his strong arm. "Something is wrong with Bea, Jake. I'll talk to Aunt Astrid tomorrow. She'll know what to do."

"I'm lost without her, Cath. I'd do anything for her. Anything. She's been acting like she hates me. Like I'm not good enough for her anymore."

To see Jake this way, so broken, it made me think of what Patience had said when she blamed me for Tom getting shot. There was some truth to that statement. A police officer who was distracted was a police officer in danger. This problem with Bea was affecting more than just her and her sense of dress. It was affecting everyone around her.

"Jake, get some rest," I said. "Even if you have to sleep on the couch. Is there any way you can call in sick tomorrow? Take a day off and go to a movie or to the gym or somewhere just to give yourself a break."

I hoped Jake would do this at least until I had a chance to talk to Aunt Astrid. She had no idea what was happening. If I knew that Jake was not at work, I'd at least be able to breathe a little easier while we got to the bottom of things.

"I can't. If I don't keep busy, I'll go crazy." He ran his hand through his hair. Just then the door to Jake's house opened, and something was tossed onto the porch. I gasped when I saw what it was.

"She threw me out!" Peanut Butter cried. *"I was just sleeping, and she picked me up by the scruff of my neck and threw me out."*

"Oh no." I hurried to the sidewalk and scooped him up. I looked at Jake, who clenched his teeth. "Jake, she's not herself. Please, don't do anything. Don't try and talk to her. Just wait until I talk to Aunt Astrid. We all need to get some sleep. I'll keep Peanut Butter until this all blows over." I nuzzled the cat as he buried his head in the crook of my arm.

"I'm going to get dressed and go into work. I can even catch forty winks there in the bullpen if I have to." He shook his head.

"Okay. Don't worry, Jake. Aunt Astrid will know what to do," I assured him. But the next morning when I walked to the café, I was surprised to see the place still locked up tight. There was no sign of Aunt Astrid.

15

SMELL OF SULFUR

Panic settled deep in my chest. I ran back to my place and grabbed Treacle and Peanut Butter before I headed across the street to my aunt's house.

"We might have to pool our magic together, guys," I said as I led the march from my house to Aunt Astrid's. I didn't want to walk into something like an ambush or attack without a little help.

"We've got your back, Cath," Treacle assured me as he marched on my right.

"I'm not afraid," Peanut Butter added.

"It's okay to be afraid, honey," I said. "It's how we act when we're afraid that counts. You look as brave as a cougar to me."

I saw Peanut Butter's shoulders square off and

his chin rise a little higher. If only I had someone to give me a pep talk like that. We went up the steps to my aunt's wide front porch. She had wind chimes with stars and moons hanging at the corner of the roof and a mat at the door that read WELCOME.

I cupped my hands over my eyes and looked in. There was no movement. Telepathically, I called Marshmallow, my aunt's Maine Coon cat, and got no answer. Finally, I rang the bell and pounded on the door.

"Aunt Astrid?" I shouted. While I pressed my ear against the cold wood, I listened for any movement.

"I'll go check out back," Treacle offered.

"I'll go with and check the back windows," Peanut Butter said.

"Okay."

I had a spare key. But the idea of using it frightened me. That meant she wasn't able to answer the door. I paced then peeked in the window again.

When Treacle and Peanut Butter returned, they said there was no sign of anyone inside. Finally, I took my key and unlocked the door. We all went inside. I could detect a strange smell of sulfur, and that was never good.

"Aunt Astrid? Hello?" I dashed upstairs while the

cats carefully circled downstairs. Finally, I heard Treacle yelling for me.

"We found them! Cath, hurry! We found them!"

I ran back down the stairs, following Treacle's voice in my head. Finally, I reached the open basement door where the two cats were standing, looking down. I saw my aunt's legs at the bottom as well as Marshmallow's. My heart caught in my throat, and tears instantly filled my eyes.

"Aunt Astrid! Marshmallow!" When I got to the bottom, I quickly inspected my aunt's head for cracks or bleeding. There was nothing. Not even a lump. I let out a great sigh of relief and scooped her head and shoulders up and into my lap.

"Aunt Astrid. Please open your eyes," I pleaded. "Please open your eyes."

For a flash, I saw Tom. I did the same thing to him, and he didn't listen. Was Aunt Astrid in a coma too? What would I do if she was? What would I tell Bea?

"Aunt Astrid, please." I shook her and smoothed her hair away from her face. I looked at her hands and saw they were dirty but not scratched or cut like she had to defend herself against something. "I need your help. Bea is in trouble. Please."

Finally, there was movement behind her closed

eyelids. Slowly, they began to flutter until finally they opened wide and she looked at me.

"Aunt Astrid? Are you all right?" I tried to smile as tears rolled down my face. This was not how I expected to start my day.

"Cath?"

"Yeah." I squeezed her to me, and I cried with relief. "What in the world happened? You gave us all such a scare. What are you doing in the basement on the floor?"

Treacle and Peanut Butter were grooming Marshmallow as she began to wake up too. I looked at the cat and asked her if she was all right.

"My back paw is hurt where she grabbed me. Other than that, I'm okay."

"Grabbed you? Who grabbed you? Aunt Astrid, what happened here?"

"It was Bea," my aunt said, pinching her lips together. I swallowed hard.

"What?" I nearly dropped my aunt's head against the concrete floor. "I just saw her last night. She said some of the strangest things. Jake came to fetch her, and she practically cussed him out in the middle of the street. Then she tossed out poor Peanut Butter."

"But I'm okay. We'll get to the bottom of this," Peanut

butter said bravely, getting affectionate head rubs from the other familiars.

"After I closed up the café and came home, I started doing some research on what we'd learned about Mrs. Kitt's death. I've narrowed it down to two possible suspects causing all the trouble. I was going to go collect you and Bea, but I saw Bea coming from the Lourdeses' house."

"Who?"

"The babe couple's house." Aunt Astrid rolled her eyes.

"Oh yeah. I'm always forgetting their real name. Wait. Why would Bea be coming from their house? Maybe she was just checking up on things for them. Believe me, I was in the house. They don't have a huge television or gaming system or even a full fridge. There is no reason for Bea to go over there. It's as boring as the post office."

"I don't know. So, I stepped outside and waved her over. I was going to ask her that very question. She was dressed so unlike herself that I knew something was very wrong. She was starting to dress like…like Mrs. Kitt had been, remember?"

"Yes, that's right." I shook my head. "Why didn't I see it before?"

"When I asked her about it, she became angry

and nasty, saying things I know my daughter would never even think, let alone utter out loud. So, in my ultimate wisdom, I tried to throw a binding spell around her quick, and I was going to go fetch you. But Bea was ready for me. I don't know how, but she was, and she tossed Marshmallow and me into the basement. I'm lucky I didn't break every bone in my body."

"So, do you think there might be a clue in the Lourdeses' house?" I asked. "Because I don't think we are going to get anywhere by asking Bea why she was there. She might have had intentions of throwing me in the basement too, but Jake came by."

I shivered at the thought. It was one thing to be attacked by a crazy entity from another dimension. It was a completely different kind of terror to have a family member do it.

"I think that is a good idea." She started to push herself up.

"Well, it's an idea, anyway. A good one? I don't know," I muttered as I helped my aunt to her feet and up the stairs.

Once we were in the kitchen, my aunt asked me to make her a special cup of tea and make sure to have some myself.

"We don't know what we are going to encounter

in there. It's just a little elixir to give us that extra protection," she said as she handed me an old tea tin with loose leaves in it.

I didn't want to say anything, but it smelled like a combination of orange and wasabi. As it turned out, it tasted like that too.

"This has got some kick," I muttered as I sipped my cup and handed Aunt Astrid hers. She had quickly changed her clothes and tied her hair up in a loose bun, with wild silver-and-red tendrils falling around her face.

"It does," she said, gulping down the hot liquid like a cowboy downing whiskey at a saloon. "Let's go."

Before we even had the front door closed behind us, Aunt Astrid took hold of my hand and pulled me close to her side. I looked at her, and she jerked her chin in the direction of the street. I followed her gaze until I saw what she was staring at. It was Bea.

❧ 16 ❧

VIAL OF SALT

Bea was running across the street from the babe couple's house back to her driveway, where she got into her car and sped down the street in the opposite direction of where we were.

"What was she doing over there?" I whispered, knowing no one had an answer. When we thought it was safe, we headed across the street to the house two doors down from mine. The front door was locked.

"How is she getting in?" I asked. "The last time we used a spell to help us pass through walls, she was puking for hours afterward. I don't think she's doing it that way, do you?"

"How did you guys get in when you needed to rescue the cats?" My aunt was shaking her head.

"We found the key at Mrs. Kitt's place. I gave it to Bea to unlock the place so Old Murray could take the cats out and then...trusted she'd lock it up and put the key back."

"Something made her keep the key in order to get inside again." My aunt looked in the window, and she looked as if she were studying something through the sheer curtains. "No. No, it can't be."

"What?" I whined.

"We need to get inside this house immediately." She looked down at the cats, who were lined up like soldiers in the army, waiting for orders. I peeked in the window but didn't see anything other than a boring love nest for the babes.

"No problem," I said as I looked at Peanut Butter. He was the youngest and the lightest of the cats and needed to start getting in the habit of assisting us witches when he could.

"Can you find a way in?" I asked him.

"I can already see a window cracked up on the third floor," he meowed proudly.

"Once you are in, do you think you can find a way to get us in?"

He looked nervously to the side but then meowed

that he'd figure something out. My aunt and I watched him shimmy up the side of the house, using the branches of trees, the bricks, and the other window ledges as his ladder. Once up on the third floor, he disappeared inside the house through the window that was only cracked about three inches.

Within seconds, he peeked out at us, with the sheer curtains making a hood over his little head.

"Good job!" I said to him. *"Do you see any window latch that you can slide open or a door handle you can turn? Anything?"*

"I'll be right back."

It was almost comical how we could hear the cat darting around from room to room, looking for a weak link in the chain.

Finally, I heard him shout he did it.

He came running back to the front window to tell us he'd opened the door to the mudroom that led to the garage.

"That's great, honey, but not exactly what we were hoping for." I slouched as I repeated his feat to my aunt.

"Oh, it isn't? Just wait," he purred.

Within seconds, the garage door started to go up. Peanut Butter strutted his stuff back and forth by the door that led into the house.

"I was wrong, kitty. Great job!" I said as my aunt and I quickly scurried inside. "Where did you learn that trick?"

"I do it at our house all the time." Peanut Butter accepted his scratches behind the ear with pride.

"That had to be something Jake taught you to do." I smiled. Jake might have been a dog man deep down, but if he was going to have a cat, that cat was going to learn some amazing tricks. Opening the garage door was pretty cool. Treacle and Marshmallow agreed as we pressed the button, sending the door back down. My initial excitement over getting inside without passing through walls or breaking a window quickly passed as I felt the oppressive air of the place.

"Now, before we go into the living room," Aunt Astrid said, "I need you to promise me something."

I looked at my aunt, who took my hands in hers.

"Anything," I said.

"Do not look in the mirrors."

"Why would I?" I asked as if she told me not to put my hand in a hill of fire ants. "I avoid mirrors at all costs. The only reason I look at the one in my house is to make sure I don't have my T-shirt on inside out."

My aunt smiled the most kind, genuine smile at

me. I didn't know why, but it was contagious, and I smiled back at her.

"We need to move those mirrors. Turn them around first and then move them," Aunt Astrid said. "Follow my instructions. We'll get this done quickly."

We walked into the living room. Even though it was a bright sunny day outside, the room was dark. There was a faint hint of sulfur in the air.

From one pocket, my aunt pulled a vial of salt. She made three tiny piles on the floor in front of each of the mirrors, five in this one room.

"There are more upstairs," I muttered. "These people love to look at themselves."

"We'll check those in a minute. These are our primary concern now," Aunt Astrid said. She clapped her hands and rubbed them together.

"*Cogitatio*. You see nothing. *Cogitatio*. You see nothing." Over and over she muttered those words as she connected the dots of salt with her fingers. With another loud clap, she rubbed her hands together.

I promised I wouldn't look at the mirrors. But as I stood in front of the big mirror Bea had been looking at, the one with the fancy frame around it, I noticed out of the corner of my eye the reflection inside bending and warping like the glass were being heated from the inside.

"Cath. Get ready to turn that mirror," Aunt Astrid ordered.

I stood next to it, awaiting her orders. My hands were cool against the frame. Aside from the mirror rolling and folding on itself, I wasn't all that scared at what we were doing. Treacle, Marshmallow, and Peanut Butter took their places, each in front of the other mirrors like guard dogs.

"*Cogitatio speculum!* Turn it! Now!"

❧ 17 ❧

BLACK MAGIC

I did as I was told and started to turn the mirror around when I felt something grab at my leg.

When I looked down, a bluish-gray gnarled arm had reached out, and the bony fingers latched onto my pants. Now I started to sweat, and my hands got slippery as I pulled the mirror.

"What is it?" I screamed.

"Don't look in the mirror, Cath! Just turn it around!" Aunt Astrid sounded like she was shouting while trying to swat away a swarm of wasps. I turned to look at her, and she, too, had arms reaching out, clawing and grabbing at her.

"What do they want? Why are they in these mirrors?"

The cats were pacing and hissing at their own mirrors as the things tried to reach for them but were stopped by the piles of purifying salt.

Treacle was hunched and fluffed to three times his size. Marshmallow was a huge cat to begin with. On the attack, he looked like a saber-tooth tiger. And I couldn't have been prouder of Peanut Butter, who was scratching and clawing at the greedy hands. But I was afraid he was getting too close.

"Peanut Butter! Back up!" I shouted just as one of those sneaky arms grabbed hold of his front paw. "NO!"

"Cath, don't let go of your mirror!" I heard my aunt cry, but the words didn't compute. I couldn't let those things get Peanut Butter.

I took three long strides across the floor, scooped him around the middle, and pulled. He bit and scratched, his tail whipping in all directions, before I dug my own fingers into the bluish-gray flesh of the creature on the other side of the mirror.

"Don't look in the mirror!" Aunt Astrid screamed.

I didn't. I didn't want to see what was in there. Finally, the arm snapped back, and Peanut Butter and I toppled backward. He jumped up and positioned himself back in front of his mirror, keeping the monsters that were now angrier than ever at bay.

When I turned to my big mirror, I was horrified to see something was crawling out of it.

As if the arms weren't gross enough, something seemed to be elongating itself as it writhed and pulled itself out of the mirror. I was only seeing it out of my peripheral vision. So, what it really looked like, I couldn't say. But from where I was standing, it was like a worm with arms and a human-shaped head, and I think it had eyes because I was pretty sure I felt them staring at me.

I jumped up, thankful for Aunt Astrid's purifying salt that kept the monster from coming all the way out, and took hold of the large mirror from the right side, trying to dislodge it from where it was positioned.

No matter how hard I pushed, my mirror seemed stuck, like a ripple of carpet or something was getting in the way. When I looked down, there were roots growing out of the bottom. They were pushing themselves into the hard wood of the floor.

"What's that?" I screamed.

"Don't look in the mirror, Cath! Just push!" Aunt Astrid yelled.

I gritted my teeth, took a deep breath, and with a

horrible, frustrated grunt, I pushed as hard as I could. Finally, something gave. I felt the roots crack and snap. The hand that had been latched onto my leg recoiled back inside the mirror, and I faced the thing to the wall.

Before I could relax, I hurried to Aunt Astrid's side and helped her turn her mirror around. The three remaining were smaller. Two hung on the wall. Quickly, we flipped them around as the hands and arms tried to swipe at us, pulling us toward our own reflections. The last one, the one on the floor where Peanut Butter stood, growling and hissing, I kicked over with my foot and was sure I heard it crack.

Finally, all the mirrors were tended to. My aunt and I both collapsed on the sofa, sweating and panting.

"What were those things in there?" I asked. "Why didn't you warn me that there were going to be skeletal hands of death attached to wormy bodies of ickiness reaching out to try and stop us?"

"Because." My aunt smoothed her hair away from her face. "Those were the easy ones. I was just glad we hadn't been too late and ran into…the big one."

"The big one? What is that?"

"The Medusa Praesentia." My aunt put her hand to her chest.

"I'm sorry. Did you just say Medusa? Like the Medusa that looks at you and turns you to stone she's so ugly?"

My aunt nodded her head. "It's nice you learned something about Greek mythology at school."

"Did we stop it?" I asked.

"I think so."

"Then I don't need to know anything more about the Medusa Praesentia. That can go on Cath's list of things I don't need to know, like algebra, basket weaving, and the life cycle of a fruit fly."

We sat in quiet for a few minutes before my aunt scared me with her next sentence.

"Okay. Are you ready to do the same thing upstairs?"

What could I say? Even if I said no, I was going to have to help. But when we got upstairs, Aunt Astrid stopped in her tracks.

"It's not up here," she said. She went along every mirror in the hallway, in the bedrooms, in the bathrooms. "It's not up here. If they had wanted the Medusa Praesentia to manifest, they'd have had to have all the mirrors working. They don't even have them laid out correctly up here."

"I'm lost," I said as the cats curled and wove back and forth along our feet.

"Those mirrors downstairs were in a specific pattern. Anyone who comes across mirrors in that pattern will get sucked in. The things they'll see, well, no need to go into all that. But every mirror in the house, and the more the better, has to be in a certain position. These are all just hung around willy-nilly. If the Lourdeses were dabbling with the Medusa Praesentia, they really did it wrong."

I snapped my fingers and rolled my eyes. "Wait! That's what the cats said!"

Now it was Aunt Astrid's turn to look at me like I was screwy.

"When I went to check on the cats, they told me that the Lourdeses had someone come in and repaint their house and rearrange all the furniture. I'm thinking they had the place redecorated so when they came home, it would be a nice surprise."

"Oh my," Aunt Astrid huffed. "If we've got some sinister interior decorators looking to work their black magic on unsuspecting homeowners one interior design at a time, well, that just boils my water."

"Careful, Aunt Astrid. Young cats are in the room."

"How do we know who did this?" my aunt huffed with her hands on her hips.

"I've got a hunch." I reached into my back pocket

and pulled out the business card I'd swiped from Mrs. Kitt's fridge. "It could be the wrong folks. But Mrs. Kitt had an appointment with them before she...you know...petrified. I saw it scheduled on her calendar. Maybe they are a totally different redecorating service, or maybe they'd know who did the Lourdeses' place. I think it's worth a shot."

Before Aunt Astrid and I left the babe couple's house, we had one last look around. We performed a quick cleaning spell, spreading a little sage smoke and some random sprinklings of salt around. The place felt light and airy when we left.

"Their place is completely devoid of anything occult or traditionally religious or even supernatural," Aunt Astrid said as she looked at their wedding picture and smiled. "Not even incense or one of those candles with the saints on them. That's weird."

"That's what I've said. They are a peculiar couple. I'd stay away at all costs."

"They aren't dangerous." My aunt rolled her eyes at me. "They are just very...blind. I think if they knew what happened here today, they'd go through great lengths to convince themselves it was all just a trick of the light."

"Some people can't handle the truth," I said.

"Let's go talk to Shesha at Nine Lemons in a Bowl. I'm interested if she can handle the truth." My aunt looked like she meant business. We had no idea what to expect from Shesha, but when we saw her, we were not surprised.

✺ 18 ✺

SHESHA

Nine Lemons in a Bowl was not in a chain of stores. It wasn't its own stand-alone store either. Nine Lemons in a Bowl was a business run from the home of Mrs. Shesha McDonald. Surprisingly, her home was quite modest, but what I saw said it wasn't quantity with this woman. It was quality.

"Can I help you laaadies?" she purred like a real live version of Catwoman. Her ensemble wasn't too far off either, as she had tight black stretch pants and a gray top of the same kind of stretchy material. Her feet were bare, and I couldn't help but notice her neck seemed abnormally long.

"Yes." Aunt Astrid introduced herself and me

before saying she'd heard through the Lourdeses that Nine Lemons in a Bowl was doing their interior decorating while they were travelling. "We were interested in the same kind of feng shui update to my home. Can we take a few moments of your time?"

Shesha gave us a sly smirk, and her right eyebrow arched as if she were not surprised in the least that her reputation had reached us. Pretending to be a lot more decrepit than she really was, Aunt Astrid took Shesha's hand. I followed behind them, taking an inventory of the stuff around the house.

"Please, come right iiin." She led us into what she called her sitting room. There was an old-fashioned desk with papers neatly piled on it. Behind it was one of those fancy chairs that was supposed to be good for your back. The windows had crystals hanging in them, as did the doorways. There were nine lemons in a bowl on the coffee table in front of where she had my aunt sit down. I casually strolled about the room. It was airy and open. But the stark white walls sort of made me feel like I was in a padded cell.

"Well, thank you. You know, feng shui isn't just a way to clear a path for positive energy, but it also invites prosperity, happiness, love. It depends on what you send out to the universe." Shesha had a strange way of talking where she stretched out some of her words like uuuniverse or cucumber waaaterrr. "I studied the fine art of feng shui in the Orient. I was a student to Master Chen."

"Master Chen?" I asked. "Can I Google him?"

"Well, you could try. But, you see, he is a bit of a luddiiite. Someone who is in opposition to technolo-gyyy. There is very little written about him onliiine. He has gone through great lengths to ensure it staaays that way."

I shrugged and nodded as if that made perfect sense. It already sounded like a big steaming pile of hoo-ha. While I strolled near the desk, I tried to peek at the papers there. I saw a contract for what looked like a design gig. There were also three unopened envelopes from the utility company, phone company, and cable company, all made out to a Miss Sally Ann McDonald. I was sure somewhere in the world someone was named Shesha, but it wasn't this woman.

While I listened politely, I watched Aunt Astrid as she studied Shesha. There was something around the woman that had her attention. I'm not sure what it was, but I couldn't wait to ask her.

"So, Shesha, do your interior design methods

incorporate any aspects of occultism or alternative religions?"

"Heavens noooo." With dramatic flourishes of her hands, she shook her head. "I follow the path of white light. That is what has brought me so much prosperity." She waved her hand around her sitting room as if to verify the results that came by hanging crystals in certain corners and placing a red area rug against a south wall and a teal-colored one against a north wall. "There is no good or eeevil. Just energyyy. I find the ideas of those things to be rather aaantiquated."

Both Aunt Astrid and I ruffled at her words. The ignorance of some people was astounding. But if she didn't believe in the supernatural, then how could she have unleashed the menace in the mirrors?

I had to admit the room we were sitting in was spotlessly white. There were amazing paintings on the walls in huge ornate frames. Fresh flowers were on almost every table. Dark oak furniture contrasted the white amazingly. I especially liked the sliding wooden doors that she had shut when we arrived. They slid into the walls. A very cool feature. But there wasn't a spot of dust anywhere. Not a drop of spilled coffee or wine. Not a sliver of chipped paint.

Not in the immediate area. But as I strolled to the back of the room, I noticed something peeking from underneath those cool sliding doors. It looked like a skid mark of mud or dirt.

"What would you charge to do an entire home of, say, seventeen hundred square feet?" I heard Aunt Astrid ask before I turned around to join the group.

"I'd have to visit the house firrrst. I let the home tell me what to charrrge."

"The home?" I asked innocently.

"You know that old saying if walls could taaalk? They speak to meee. They tell me where the pain is. Where the blockage is. Where things are moving freely and where they arrren't." She folded her hands in her lap and looked at me. "Once I assess the injuries, I can listen for the feee. It comes to me quite clearlyyy."

I'm sure it did. I wasn't as intuitive as Aunt Astrid or Bea, but I was having a hard time believing what this woman said. If she was the mastermind behind unleashing the Medusa thingamabob in the Lourdeses' home, I was a monkey's aunt.

"Do you have anyone else working with you?" my aunt asked.

"I have a pool of contractorrrs, painterrrs, who do

the heavy lifting for me." She put her hand to her chest. "But I am the sole designer. Well, my husband does help at times. He's also highly skilled in feng shui, but he's participating in a convention circuit that has been moving for the past few months. Every week, he's travelling to a different part of the countryyy. He'll be baaack in two more weeeks."

"What about mirrors?" I asked. "Do you think they are good or bad for feng shui?"

"I think they are wonderful, if not key, to successful energy transitioning. In fact, I'd say the more the beeetter. They not only reflect the good vibrations, but they do help make a space look bigger. Plus, who doesn't want to see more of themseeelves?" She laughed, but nothing came out except a high-pitched sigh.

After a few more questions, my aunt took one of Shesha's business cards and promised to call as soon as she decided if she was really going to have her home redecorated.

"Please, understand that time is of the esseeence," Shesha said without smiling. "My schedule is booked for the next several mooonths. I can keep you on standby for anyone who caaancels. Otherwise, it may not be until the new year before I can get to you."

"I'll take that into consideration, Shesha. Thank you again for your time." Aunt Astrid held onto my arm as we left the lovely sitting room, crossed the foyer, and were just about out the front door when she turned around.

"I'm sorry to bother you, Shesha, but I have one more question. May I use your bathroom?" I looked at my aunt Astrid. It wasn't that I doubted she needed to use the bathroom, but something in her tone of voice sounded funny to me.

"Oh...um...of courrrse." Shesha looked a bit disturbed by the request.

How could she not expect someone to have to use the can at her business when her business was in her house? That was the price she had to pay for skimping on rent at a regular shop. At least, that was my opinion on the matter.

"Just follow meee."

Aunt Astrid motioned for me to stay behind, and I got a vibe that she wanted me to just have a little lookie-loo while Shesha was escorting her to the bathroom. I walked across the parlor to the closed doors that slid into the walls and cracked them just an inch.

I didn't know what I was expecting. A black room with red pentagrams painted on the floor and walls or maybe a torture chamber or maybe even a room full of mirrors that were in the same crazy pattern as the mirrors at the Lourdeses' house. Instead, I saw a messy living room with take-out boxes and soda bottles on almost every flat surface. There were a few pieces of clothing on the floor. The curtains were drawn so no one could see in. The skid marks on the ground led to a pair of dirty gym shoes.

When I thought I heard the pat of Shesha's feet on the floor, I quickly closed the door and stepped in front of one of the large paintings she had. Wherever she'd gotten it, it was very pretty.

"That's a silk desiiign from Master Chen's priiivate collection. He gave that to me when I left the Orient."

"Asia is someplace I'd love to see someday," I said. "Where were you, exactly?"

"Oh, well, it's hard to say. You see the study of feng shui is not something that can be learned in a classroom. It is an exercise in the freeing of the mind and opening oneself up to the direction of the positive energies around uuus."

What a load of bull, I thought.

Just then my aunt showed up. She reached her hand out for to me. Once she took hold, she thanked Shesha again, and we left.

When we were off the Nine Lemons in a Bowl property and safely driving down the street back toward the café, I looked over at my aunt.

"What's your opinion?"

"That is one of the biggest con artists I've ever seen," Aunt Astrid said. "Feng shui is a lovely concept, and some people do find benefits in rearranging their furniture this way or that. But that woman is no more qualified to be arranging people's interiors than the man on the moon."

I reported to my aunt what I saw in the other room. There was a definite "no feng shui zone" going on in there.

"The more that woman talked, the more I could see the shifting levels of comfort around her. We were making her very uncomfortable," Aunt Astrid said.

"Why? I thought we were being pleasant as punch."

"I think she was afraid we were going to ask that one question she didn't know the answer to and discover she was a fraud," she said.

"I'm finding it hard to believe the babe couple fell for this. They paid to have this woman work her magic in their home. The place looks like a furniture showroom." I chuckled. "So, what does it all mean?"

"It means that she arranged those mirrors in that house and accidentally called the Medusa Praesentia," Aunt Astrid said. "The really sad thing is that this could happen again. The chances are slim that she'd get the exact same positioning, but what are the chances it even happened this one time?"

"Okay, well, now what do we do? We've still got to check in with Bea and make sure she's all right. You think since we turned the mirrors around and shifted things up, that she's back to normal?"

"That's my hope." Aunt Astrid seemed calm about the situation, but I had a weird tickle in my belly that was making me think that it couldn't be that easy.

"So, back to the café? We're losing business," I suggested. "Plus, if Bea is better, she's probably wondering where we are."

Aunt Astrid nodded. Her calm made me uneasy. I couldn't say why. I wished the cats were with us so that I could talk with them and see what they were sensing. But after the showdown, I was determined they were going to stay together at my house and rest. Just in case we needed their help again.

I let out a deep sigh and drove to the café. There was movement inside, but the lights were still off, the Closed sign was up, and it wasn't Kevin, our baker, who had suddenly dyed his hair red.

"What's Bea doing in there?" I asked.

When we pulled up, got out of the car, and walked up to the door, we couldn't believe what we were seeing.

REFLECTION

Bea was wearing a horrible leopard-printed dress that looked like it came off the rack from a stripper's dressing room. Aunt Astrid and I both gasped as we saw she was cleaning out the cash register. With trembling hands, my aunt unlocked the door.

"Bea? What are you...?"

"Shut up. I don't want to hear it." She rolled her eyes and continued to put the money in her purse.

"Honey, if you need money, I'll give it to you. You don't have to steal it," my aunt said as she inched closer.

I had to pull my chin up off the floor after hearing her tell my aunt, her mother, to shut up. Had I not been out of arm's reach, I would have slapped her myself.

"This has gone on long enough." I stomped up to Bea and snatched her purse from her hand. "What do you think you're doing?"

Okay. Yes. I suddenly regretted that move when Bea glared at me. I thought I was going to turn to stone right then and there. And that was when the reality of what was going on sank in. We didn't get rid of anything. We might have closed one portal, but this was far from over.

"Give that back, or I'll scratch your eyes out," she hissed at me.

"You give it your best shot, cuz." I handed the purse to my aunt to take the money out. My knees were shaking, and I didn't have a drop of saliva in my mouth. But I wasn't the one who blinked first.

"Do you really think I'm scared of you? You are an ugly girl who can't get a husband and will grow old with her cat. You don't have what I have." She strutted past me like a streetwalker. "I'm getting out of here, and you can't stop me."

"Bea. What about Jake? He loves you," Aunt Astrid interrupted. "We all do."

"Jake?" She laughed. "Jake is just a stepping stone."

That was when I noticed it again. She was looking at her reflection as she spoke. In the glass of the windows. In the toaster. In the mirror behind the counter. Anywhere she could catch a glimpse of herself, she was looking, and she didn't seem to notice she had gaudy, tacky makeup on in addition to the too-tight dress she was wearing. She had a cute figure but not cute enough she could wear something two sizes too small. Not to mention about ten years too young.

"Don't you hear yourself, Bea?" I asked. "You don't talk like that. You love Jake. You guys are the poster children for Valentine's Day."

"Ha. Look at me. I deserve better than Jake and all of you. Now get out of my way." She nearly knocked her mother to the ground as she stomped out of the café, got in her car, and sped off.

"Should we follow her?"

"No. I know where she's going." My aunt started to cry as I helped her get her balance. "We were too late. The Medusa Praesentia has infected her. Come on. We need to find out exactly what to do to stop this, or Bea is going to suffer the same fate as Mrs. Kitt."

Those words were like ice water down the middle of my spine. "How long do you think we have?"

"I don't think we have twenty-four hours." My aunt wiped her eyes and then hurried down into the bunker. "I just need to get a couple of books. Then we need to go back to your house."

"My house? Why my house?" That was a strange request because all the supplies, all the books and journals and maps, were at my aunt's house.

"Because Bea's going to the babe couple's house, and she'll be very angry when she realizes what we've done."

She emerged from the steps with several thick books in her arms. I took four of them, and she carried the remaining three as we left the café, putting the Closed sign up and locking the place up tight. Aunt Astrid quickly muttered a security spell on the door to make sure Bea didn't get back in.

"We need to get Jake here," she said as I sped to my front door.

"I'll call him." We piled out and were greeted by our cats, rested and ready for more. "How are you guys feeling?"

They meowed and rubbed against my aunt and me as we came inside.

"Is everything okay?" Treacle asked.

"No. Bea is sick." I looked at all the cats, especially Peanut Butter. *"We've got to help her. She's in grave*

danger, and we don't have a lot of time. I'll need you guys to be ready to pounce at our mark, even if it is at Bea. Do you understand? If we don't, she could hurt herself or one of us."

My aunt hurried to the kitchen, where I followed her. I picked up my phone and called the police station to get ahold of Jake. When he picked up the phone, he sounded like he'd been crying too.

I knew it was selfish, but for an instant, I thought something had happened to Blake. They'd been partners for some time, and if they went on a call and Blake was hurt or worse, I was going to swear off cops forever and join a convent.

"Jake, it's Cath. What happened?"

"You mean Bea didn't tell you?" He cleared his throat.

"Tell us what?" I took hold of Aunt Astrid's hand and squeezed.

"She wants a divorce." I could tell he was trying to put on a brave face in front of the other officers. But my heart was breaking for him.

"No, she doesn't!" I yelled. "Jake, she's sick."

"Yeah. Sick of me. That's what she said." There was anger there too. I thought that was good because, as long as Jake was a bit ticked off, we could talk sense into him. Despair was the real enemy.

"Jake. You've got to get to my place right away. I

mean right now!" I barked into the phone. "Look, I'm just going to blurt this out. Don't expect it to make sense. But she's under a kind of spell. It was an accident."

"You put her under a spell?" I heard him clench his teeth.

"Of course I didn't. Jake! Just get over here! Aunt Astrid will explain everything. But you've got to hurry because you remember old Mrs. Kitt with the rock-hard innards? Well, Bea is going to be joining her in the petrified Miss America contest if we don't get moving."

He agreed, and within minutes, I heard his car tires squealing in the driveway. He let himself in, and I swear I never saw a more pitiful sight in my life. It looked as if he hadn't slept in about a week. I thought he lost weight too. His shirt was wrinkled, and so were his pants.

My aunt and I had several of her spell books open on the kitchen table, each one of them displaying a creature more gruesome than the last.

"Jake." Aunt Astrid took his hand. "Bea is under the spell of the Medusa Praesentia." She pointed to the thing in the book.

Jake blinked, but it was obvious his mind was not at one hundred percent, and he was struggling just to remain standing, let alone comprehend anything so outside this world.

When my aunt showed me the picture, I had to admit I wanted to run out of my house and down the street, screaming. But of course, I stayed. I went into my bedroom and took a photo off my dresser. It was one of Bea and me last Christmas. We'd just handled another bugaboo and were able to relax with food and drinks and Christmas music, and someone, I don't know who, snapped our picture. Bea was beautiful, with her red hair curling around her face, and I had to admit I looked nice in a green dress I'd found. But more importantly, we were comfortable around each other enough to smile wide and hold hands like sisters.

She would never talk to me the way she had if there wasn't something wrong. And I wasn't going to let the other world, the one divided by that thin veil, sink its claws into her. No matter how scary and big it looked.

"The Medusa Praesentia is a vanity spirit," my aunt said as she took notes from the book.

"Vanity? Bea isn't vain," Jake snapped. "She's one of the humblest people I've ever met."

"Of course she is, Jake!" my aunt snapped. "But the Medusa Praesentia doesn't care what she's like in real life. It showed her a flawless reflection. Once Bea saw it, she couldn't look away. Have you ever imagined what would happen if you saw yourself as perfect?"

I looked at Jake and then back at my aunt. The conversation had become awkward.

"Imagine it, Jake. No physical flaws, even the tiniest thing that only you focus on. You'd be in perfect shape. Your body would look better than anyone else's around you. And once you looked perfect, you'd start to see the flaws in everyone else more clearly. They'd seem uglier, dirtier. Even those you love would become ignorant and unclean in your eyes. You'd want nothing to do with them. And the more you looked at the beauty you'd become, the less you'd want to see the lepers your loved ones had become."

"It's like a reverse Dorian Gray," I sputtered. "Except you're getting uglier on the inside literally and figuratively."

"That's right!" My aunt pointed at me. "Cath, I need some twine, sage, and how many white candles do you have?"

"You always said have a minimum of six. So, I've got six." I sighed.

"That'll work. Get them," she ordered.

I went underneath the kitchen sink and pulled them out and set them with all the books on my table.

"The problem with seeing yourself as perfect and everyone else as flawed is that it starts to harden your heart. So much so that in the simple chest of a human, the tissue just can't take it. The blood no longer pumps. Oxygen is no longer there. A person has turned so inward, they kill themselves without even realizing it until it's too late."

"This is what happened to Bea?" Jake paled.

"Yes," my aunt said. "How? Through a freak accident when she happened to gaze into a mirror that was infected with the parasite. Plus, her being an empath made her an even more irresistible host. But it is that same power that I believe has kept her alive long enough for us to figure this out and come up with a plan."

"What is the plan?" I asked.

"We have to go next door to the Lourdeses' house and face the Medusa Praesentia."

"Oh no. Do we have to cut off its head? Like in the movies? You have to cut off Medusa's head in order to kill her? Whose gonna do that?" I whimpered.

"I'll do it," Jake said without hesitating. I was glad. That sounded like men's work if I ever heard it.

"No. We don't have to cut off its head. I have a better idea," Aunt Astrid said. "We'll give it a taste of its own medicine."

"Okay, I don't know what that means," I blubbered. "But I'm scared. I'm scared that this is not going to be the end of things, and what happens if we look at our reflections this time? I mean, what do we do if we all get sucked into the vanity universe?"

"That's another thing." Aunt Astrid took Jake's hands in hers. "Jake, whatever you do, don't look in the mirrors."

"What?" He shook his head.

"Don't look in the mirrors, Jake!" I shouted. "Come on. Get your head in the game! We've got to save Bea!"

"Right," Jake muttered, and I saw his eyes clear and look at Aunt Astrid. "Right. What do you need me to do?"

🦋 20 🦋

A MIRROR INFECTED

We looked like a cleaning crew heading over to the Lourdeses' house. Peanut Butter worked his magic again, letting us all in through the garage door. By this time, the sun was starting to set. We came into the house that was just as we had left it. The feeling of peace and openness still hung in the air even though it was getting darker inside.

"How do you know Bea is going to come?" Jake asked.

"She has to," Aunt Astrid said. "That's one of its hooks. It shows the victim what perfection looks like. The victim then thinks they can go and get love, money, sex, whatever, because they are seeing the perfection.

But the truth is doubt always sets in. It drags them back to the mirror every time, and only a mirror infected with the Medusa Praesentia will show them what they want to see. They are chained to it. Slaves to it."

It reminded me of a movie I saw with Frank Sinatra, and he was a heroin addict. He had talent and someone who loved him, and he tossed it all away. This was no different.

"Jake, I need you to move that mirror over there to that window," Aunt Astrid instructed. She told me to place the white candles on the floor in front of each mirror. "But keep them slightly out of the way. I don't want Bea to see them and get tipped off we are here."

"Where are we going to be?" I asked.

"Hiding until the very last moment," Aunt Astrid said as she burned sage again and then made a string of knots from the twine. "Cath, we need to do a protection spell. Marshmallow, Treacle, Peanut Butter. All of you. We need this to be a good one. If that thing tries to get into this world, we need to be able to stop it."

Jake stared at us as we recited a protection spell calling on the four corners of the earth, the seasons, the sun and moon as well as the grand designer of the whole universe who created everything from the biggest whale to the tiniest amoeba.

It was a strong spell that filled the space. I could feel it as I walked, like I was travelling in the direction of a soothing breeze.

The cats were told to stay out of sight until they were needed.

"Cath, there is just one last thing we need to do," Aunt Astrid said. "Jake, you need to let us do a special protection spell over you. You are going to be the one closest to the mirror."

"I understand, Astrid." He put his hand on her shoulder. "I won't look."

"I know you'll do your best. But it will be calling you. We need to blind you, temporarily."

I gasped when I heard my aunt's suggestion.

"I can't do that." He shook his head.

"You've got to trust me, Jake. It's for your own good."

"But how is that going to help Bea?" He looked at me for backup. I was struck dumb and just kept my mouth shut as I walked over to the window and peeked out the sheer curtains. That's when I saw her car.

"Guys?"

"It is temporary, Jake. You've got to trust me."

"Guys?" I said again as Bea climbed out of her car.

"Mom, I promise. I won't look at the mirror."

"Guys!" I barked. "She's back, and she's coming this way!"

Before Jake could do anything, my aunt waved her hands over his eyes.

"Visus disunate," she whispered and took both his hands. "Trust me, Jake. You'll see her. You'll see her like you've never seen her before. Just tell her you love her. No matter what she says."

Aunt Astrid took Jake by the hands and led him to a closet where she tucked him away, leaving the door open slightly. He was to call Bea once he heard her voice. Aunt Astrid hid behind the curtains on the other wall. I stood behind the tall mirror we'd moved.

The entire place was as quiet as a tomb. Bea's footsteps up the walk were the only sound I heard. She sounded angry as she fumbled with the keys in the lock. I had a strange image pop into my mind. Wouldn't it just ruin everything if the Lourdeses were to come home now? We'd all be arrested. Bea would probably be dead. Poor Jake wouldn't be able to see until it was too late. It would be like a Marx Brothers' movie.

Finally, Bea came in. She dropped her things and ran in my direction. She stared into the mirror. She just stood there, looking like she was waiting for something.

"Where?" She shifted from one foot to the other. "Where is it?" She tugged at her hair and adjusted her dress. But her face was becoming more and more wrinkled. She was getting upset. Her breath was coming in shorter gasps.

She turned and went to the other mirror that was on the other side of the room. She stared into that one the same way.

"What's happening?" she whispered to herself. "Where is it?"

"Bea?" Jake stepped out of the closet.

"Ugh! What are you doing here?" she whined as he emerged from the closet, his hands stretched out in front of him. "What have you done with it?"

"Done with what?" he asked.

"What have you done? You had to have done something! You ruined this! You ruined it just like you've ruined everything else. I don't know how I could stand to look at you for so long!" Bea shouted.

It broke my heart.

"I love you, Bea. I've loved you since the minute I

first saw you. I knew that you were going to be my wife," he said as he inched his way closer.

"Get out of here, Jake!"

"Neither one of us should be here, Bea. This isn't our house."

"You shut up! Just shut up! You ruined it! I saw after all these years what I really am, and I don't know why I ever settled for someone like you. Pity, I guess."

"You don't mean that," he said calmly. It was then that I could hear a strange sound. There was a weird humming noise that was hovering around the periphery of us.

I saw Aunt Astrid emerge from behind the curtains. Just as she did, Bea headed toward the front door, but Jake was able to grab her. I didn't know how he knew to do it. But he caught her quick and snapped her up. He held her tightly in his strong arms, her back to his chest, as she yelled and kicked and thrashed to get free.

"Let go of me! I hate you! Do you understand that? I hate you both! You disgust me! Let me go!" she screamed.

"Take her in front of the mirror, Jake," Aunt Astrid said. "Cath, get the sage burning, and make sure you've got a flame on each white candle."

As soon as she said my name, Bea really let loose.

"Cath! Don't you do it! Get me out of here, Cath!"

"Bea, we're trying to help you. Just relax in the arms of the man you love, and this will all be over soon," I said without looking anywhere but my task at hand.

"You're worthless," she started. "Look at you. I can't believe anyone would ever want to be around you. How Blake can be in love with you I have no idea. You're disgusting."

At the mention of Blake and the word love, I looked up at Bea. She didn't even resemble my cousin. She was filled with vile conceit and disgust for everything around her. It wasn't her at all. But she said those words, and now I was distracted. My hand trembled, and one of the candles just wouldn't light.

"Cath! Get the home fires burning!" Aunt Astrid yelled.

"I'm trying," I muttered. The wick was too small. It wasn't catching. Just as I picked it up to roll it over an open flame and melt some of the wax, all the cats started hissing.

"It's coming, Cath!" Treacle warned.

"I'm hurrying!" I said. This wick wouldn't light.

"I love you so much, Bea." Jake did as Aunt Astrid instructed. It was obvious every word came from his heart. The more he spoke, the harder she fought. "I was willing to let your mom blind me. And you know what? She was right. I can see you better now than I ever could before. You are beautiful. You have something in your heart that glows. It's your gift. I've seen it. I've seen how you can help people, and only an angel from heaven could do what you do. Oh, Bea. You are my whole world. I love you more than you'll ever know."

"Cath! Get that candle lit!" my aunt screamed. I dripped the wax around the wick onto the floor. Finally, the flame took hold of the little tip and glowed blue and then orange.

But it was too late. Something was coming through the mirror. Aunt Astrid, whose eyes had rolled back, white in her head, stood in front of the full-length mirror just beyond the line of knotted twine.

I wanted to look in the mirror. Something was pulling my face toward it, but I fought. Instead, I turned my head and saw it out of the corner of my eye. It was that same bluish-gray color. Except this thing was bigger. A hoof came out first. Then I saw what looked like a sagging belly and thin, old breasts hanging low.

I didn't see its face. I felt it looking at me, pulling my eyes toward it, but I didn't look. Bea was screaming and kicking. I didn't know if she saw the thing or not.

"That one is mine." The voice was lovely, like a song.

"No. She isn't. Medusa Praesentia! Go back to the dimension you came from!" my aunt yelled. I saw her pick up one of the mirrors and hold it up in front of her. But before she could catch the thing in its own reflection, it knocked her to the ground. The mirror shattered into a thousand pieces.

"That one has a gift. She's mine." A hand appeared at the mirror and started to pull the rest of the creature out from the portal.

❧ 21 ❧

FALLEN

"No! She isn't!" I yelled.

Treacle and Marshmallow attacked the thing, their fur standing on edge, their cries sounding wild. It was just enough of a distraction for me to yank the smallest mirror from the wall and hold it up in front of my face as I stood toe-to-toe with the Medusa Praesentia.

I was like a Lilliputian compared to this thing. But I squeezed my eyes shut as I held the mirror up in my trembling hands. Everything in the house froze. I could smell sulfur. Never a good sign. I waited for some giant claw to swat me into the wall or teeth to sink into my head. Nothing happened.

"Aunt Astrid?" There was no reply. "Bea?"

I opened my eyes and made sure they were

looking at the floor. Except, there was no floor. I looked up, and I was still holding the mirror.

The thing with the hooves and the wilting skin was still in front of me. Its hands were dangerously close to mine, holding the mirror. It was caught in its own hideous gaze.

When I looked behind me, I saw the Lourdeses' living room. I saw Aunt Astrid screaming. Bea had collapsed, and Jake, who couldn't see, was holding her in his arms. Treacle was standing there, staring at me.

I've fallen into the mirror, I thought. *How did that happen?*

I didn't know, but if I didn't do something, the Medusa Praesentia was going to realize I was on the other side of the mirror, and well, I didn't want to think of what it was going to do. Did I let go and try and swim or run to the opening? Or did I hold on and risk that thing seeing me?

Holding on quickly became a bad idea, as the Medusa Praesentia was falling farther and farther into darkness. The mirror fell aside, and I saw its face.

I gasped, but still there was no sound. Its eyes were huge circles set wide on a head that looked too heavy for the thin neck to support. It had more than one row of pointy teeth and a narrow chin. Spreading up from its back over its head were smaller heads with fangs and wide eyes set far apart.

"So that's why they called it Medusa," I muttered.

It looked like the drawings in my aunt's book. Except those had no color. It was sickly looking. Blue like it was choking or had succumbed to hypothermia. Its body twitched and jerked as it continued to stare at itself. And then I watched as its petrification started.

I knew I should have just looked away and started pushing my way back toward my family. The smaller heads on the big head started to crack. It was like they were drying up from the inside out. Just like Mrs. Kitt's heart.

At the same time, the hooves were also drying up. Everything was cracking and snapping. As it started to crack in the middle, I decided I'd seen enough. There was a strange glow coming from deep inside the thing, and I didn't want to be around to see what happened once it consumed the entire body.

I turned myself in this weird, freefalling space and tried to run toward my family. The opening was smaller than it had been. Either it was shrinking, or I was falling farther and farther away.

All around me was the most pitch-black darkness I'd ever seen. It was like a cloth that blocked out every shred of light. It was becoming suffocating. It was going to drown me if I didn't hurry.

Treacle sat at the edge, looking in at me. Could he see me? I wasn't sure. I started to windmill my arms like I was swimming. I pushed my legs, making my thighs burn. Still the hole seemed to be getting smaller. I looked behind me, and the Medusa Praesentia blinked one evil eye as it began its half-dead pursuit. I opened my mouth to scream, but nothing came out. I couldn't even be sure there was air in this place.

My heart began to pound so loudly that the blood rushing in my veins sounded like a raging waterfall. Tears stung my eyes, and I stretched and pushed myself farther as the thing reached its bony, almost-dead arm out to me.

Its fingers curled and uncurled as if it were pushing itself closer and closer to me. A forked blue tongue licked its rows of teeth just as it cracked and began to fall off into pieces. I looked to where the mirror was. I was never going to make it.

I took one last look at Aunt Astrid. Bea was still

unconscious in Jake's arms. I hoped she wouldn't blame herself for this, like I'd done over my mother for so long. It wasn't her fault.

Then I looked at Treacle. He was no longer sitting. He was up on his hind legs. I could see his little mouth meowing, but I couldn't hear what he was saying. Aunt Astrid would take good care of him.

I felt hot breath on the back of my neck. I didn't want to turn around, but something said I needed to face this evil.

As I peered over my shoulder, the Medusa Praesentia was riddled with cracks that were pulsing and growing brighter and brighter as it reached for me. They spread out and pushed its body into painfully contorted angles until, finally, in a silent instant, it exploded.

The force of the blast sent me hurtling toward the opening. Before I could stop myself, I broke through a slimy, thin membrane and crashed onto the Lourdeses' living room floor with a splat.

"Cath!" Aunt Astrid cried as she hobbled over to me. "Oh, Cath! I thought I lost you! My sweet darling girl!"

She knelt down on the floor next to me and scooped me into her arms.

I'd hit my head on impact. But I was able to sit up. Treacle wedged himself in between Aunt Astrid and me. He butted his head against my chin, his motor sounding more like a Harley than just his purring.

"What did you think you were doing?" he asked as he proceeded to get slime all over himself.

"I don't even know," I replied telepathically as I rubbed my forehead and felt the goose egg that was developing there. *"How long was I in there?"*

"Too long. You had me scared. Let's not do that again. Don't go where I can't follow." He went back and forth on my chin and cheek before I kissed him and assured him I was all right.

"Promise," I replied and looked at Jake and Bea.

"Cath. You saved her," Jake stammered. His eyes didn't see, but they were shedding tears all the same. He reached his hand out to me, and I took hold of it.

"Sorry about the mess," I said as he recoiled from the slime. "I sneezed in my hand."

"What?"

"Don't listen to her, Jake." Aunt Astrid was laughing with relief. Tears were in her eyes too, but they were more relieved than anything else. That is, until she looked at Bea.

"Can we get out of this creepy house?" I asked,

slowly getting to my knees and using the couch to pull myself up. "I know we did some damage here, but can't we just let it go for now?"

"We're going to have to," my aunt said. "We need to get Bea home. Jake, can you walk?"

"Yes, ma'am," he said bravely.

"Good. You carry her. Cath and I will lead you to your house. She'll need to rest." Aunt Astrid also got to her feet and dusted the debris from her skirt. "This is gross, Cath."

"I know, right?" I ran my hand over my head and came away with a handful of goo. "Do I have to worry about this? I'm not going to grow a third eye or come down with shingles because of this stuff, am I?"

"I don't think the astral membrane between dimensions causes any illnesses. If it did, we wouldn't have vampires, bigfoot, chupacabras, and the like," Aunt Astrid said as she helped lead Jake out of the house.

"Mom, can you take a picture of Cath for me?" Jake asked as he stood, with Bea in his arms. "I'd like to see what I'm missing."

"Okay, that's a nice thing to say," I blurted out as I steered him by the shoulders from behind. It was dark outside. Most of the neighborhood houses had their porch lights on. It gave us enough light to see by but kept the gory details of our sorry state hidden from prying eyes.

Treacle stayed close by my side, but I saw the fearful look on Peanut Butter's face and could sense it from his body language.

"Don't worry, Peanut. Aunt Astrid says she'll be all right," I soothed.

"She doesn't look all right."

I looked at Bea, and to be honest, Peanut Butter was right. She still had all that heavy makeup on. It had run down her face, making her look like she'd spent the last hour in a sauna.

"We just need to clean her up," I added. *"You'll see. Plus, she's been through so much. Her body is going to need time to recover. But she'll be back to herself in no time."*

"Promise?" The cat looked up at me innocently.

"I promise."

"Plus, we won't leave her side," Marshmallow added as she came up to Peanut Butter and walked protectively next to him. *"We'll keep her warm and share our life force with her. We've got energy to spare. Besides, she's just exhausted. She's not in a coma."*

"Oh no!" I cried and put my hand to my chest. "Jake, before you came over, did you hear anything more about Tom?"

"No, Cath. As far as I know, there's no change," he said as Aunt Astrid told him to be careful going up the porch steps. He counted them, planting both feet firmly on each step before advancing to the next one. We all piled into the house.

"Do you need to set her down and take a rest?" Aunt Astrid asked. "You can set her on the couch and—"

"No, Mom. I've been trying to hold her in my arms for the past couple of days. It feels good. I can carry her." He ascended the stairs to their bedroom as if he were carrying nothing more than a basket of clean laundry. Even blind, he was determined to take care of her. That made my stomach twist, but I kept the sour feeling to myself.

"Jake, mind if I use your shower?" I asked quietly as he laid Bea down on the bed. "I've got to get this stuff off me."

"Of course, Cath. Anything you need," he said as he snuggled in next to her.

As I walked out of the room, I heard my aunt whispering a reversal spell over Jake. It would just be about twenty minutes and his eyesight would return.

I flipped on the light and looked in the mirror before shutting the door. I was covered in bluish-gray snot from head to toe.

"Well, these clothes will go in the garbage. In fact…" I talked to myself as I peeled off my clothes and hopped underneath the hot spray of water from the shower. "Maybe they should be burned. Just to be on the safe side."

I nodded to myself. I was trying to focus on anything and everything that didn't have to do with Tom. I'd forgotten about him. I totally forgot that my boyfriend was in the hospital in a coma. What kind of person was I?

Leave it to Bea to have half a dozen different shampoos and body soaps that all smelled like either lavender or cherry blossoms. I grabbed the one that was closest, squeezed a handful out, and slapped it on my head. While I worked up a lather, I felt the slime quickly leaving my hair. Thankfully, my hair was still staying in my head.

"Can I come in?" my aunt called from outside the bathroom door.

"Sure?" I wrinkled my nose. What in the world did she need while I was in the shower?

"Is all that stuff coming off?" she asked.

"It seems to be," I admitted as I rubbed my arms with the lather from my head. "How are Bea and Jake?"

"Bea hasn't woken up yet. I don't suspect she will

for quite some time. Her body has to heal itself. Unfortunately, she is the only empath I know. If I knew of another one, I'd have them here in an instant."

"And Jake?" I asked.

"He's worried, but he's in the bed next to her, talking sweetly to her. That helps." Those words stung, and I cried under the water falling down but didn't say anything to my aunt about it.

"Cath, I'm so proud of you," my aunt said. "I didn't even realize your other gift. I'm so sorry. I guess I've known you for so long that I take some of your characteristics for granted."

"Okay. You aren't making any sense, Auntie," I said from behind Bea's pink shower curtain. "But that's okay."

"No. Your other gift. I'm sorry I never acknowledged it."

"That makes two of us because I don't know what you are talking about." I rolled my eyes. I was throwing myself quite a pleasant little pity party over my forgetfulness and bad-girlfriend characteristics. My aunt barging in to tell me how wonderful I was wasn't fitting with the theme.

"I assumed we all needed to cover our eyes from the Medusa Praesentia. We would see ourselves and fall in love like we do on a much smaller scale every day when we get dressed. But you don't ever look at yourself, do you?" My aunt had taken a seat on the toilet.

"I mean, if I've eaten any of Bea's spinach salad, I do just to make sure I don't gross anyone out." I shrugged as I wiped myself off with a soapy loofa.

"No. What I mean is you are humble. You didn't get caught by the mirror, because you don't care to look in them. And when you went into the vortex, you didn't see the horror of your vanity in the Medusa Praesentia. Nothing was going to turn you to stone." She said it proudly. "It almost tore you limb from limb, but it could never petrify your heart. Your heart beats with too much life."

"I don't know about all that, Aunt Astrid." I let the tears fall since no one would know the difference. "I forgot about Tom. That sounds like a pretty selfish person to me."

"Why? You think you are selfish because you wanted to help your cousin who you've known your whole life? You wanted to help the one person you know could help him?"

"Oh gosh! See? I forgot about that!" I whined. "I forgot Bea's gift could help him! I forgot that she could help unwrap whatever might be keeping him in that dark place. What's wrong with me?" I splashed more water on my face.

"Cath, you act like we just went for a walk in the park. If you didn't focus on the task at hand, we could have lost Bea." She cleared her throat. "I like Tom. But he isn't like Jake. Sometimes we have to pick."

"You know how people are, Aunt Astrid. A boyfriend is in the hospital, you drop everything and put life on hold and stay at the hospital for hours and hours until he's in the clear. I barely gave him a pep talk, let alone made any kind of effort to visit every day."

I looked at my fingers, making sure none of that blue stuff was caught around my cuticles or under my nails.

"Well, let's not forget about Patience. You did have a bit of a roadblock in your way." I shrugged at Aunt Astrid's reply. "You know, Cath, I've heard people say they would die for their significant other. I hear Bea and Jake say it. And although it's a beautiful concept, no one ever says they will live for their significant other. You are an example of someone who lives for who they love."

She stood up and opened the door. She didn't know that I didn't love Tom anymore. That I'd just woken up one day and didn't feel the same anymore. How could I tell her? She loved Tom.

"Whether that love be the real deal or whether it is more brotherly, you live for the people you love. I think that is a great gift too." She stepped out of the bathroom. "Oh, and Jake says don't use all the hot water."

I chuckled as my aunt pulled the door shut. I'd decided to hang around until Bea was awake. Little did I know how long that would take.

✺ 22 ✺

SAY HIS NAME

"**W**here's my cat?"

I saw Treacle lounging lazily on the mantel of Bea's fireplace when I came downstairs from my shower wearing one of Bea's cozy sweat suits.

"Don't tell me you cleaned yourself," I said to Treacle. *"We don't know what that slime was. I think you need a bath."*

"I don't need a bath."

"Ugh. Of course you do. If you digest that stuff, it might change you into a horrifying monster or maybe even a dog."

"I don't need a bath, Cath."

"Yes, you do. Now we can do this the easy way or the hard way. You decide."

Treacle didn't like the water. But he slowly

stretched, yawned, and finally hopped off the mantel and followed me into the bathroom, where I filled the sink with a little warm water.

"See, you don't even have too much of this stuff on you," I soothed as he hopped up on the counter.

"*What are we going to do now?*" he asked, closing his bright-green eyes as I took a washrag, wet it with a little water, added soap, and gently stroked his fur where the goop had started to dry.

"*Well, I think we should wait around until Bea wakes up. But I don't have any idea when that will be. Why? What were you thinking?*"

"*I was just asking.*"

"*Do you mind being here?*" I asked him.

"*No.*"

"*You sound like something is on your mind, big kitty.*"

"*We're missing someone,*" Treacle said and looked up at me. He adored Tom, and I knew he missed seeing him.

"*Tom is still in the hospital. For as good a girlfriend as I am, he could be dead, and I wouldn't know it.*"

I stroked him as I watched him shrink in size as the water matted down his fur. He looked like a little kitten again.

"*I wasn't talking about Tom.*"

"Really? Who were you talking about?" I asked

aloud. I knew exactly who Treacle was talking about and felt funny even entertaining the thought of calling Blake Samberg to come over here at a time like this.

"What are you getting all upset about? I didn't say anything."

"I'm not upset. I just don't think that thinking of myself right now is the right idea. Plus, what would I tell him? And look at me. I'm in Bea's sweats. And believe it or not, these pastel-pink things were the least girly-girl pair she had. I look like a cream puff."

"What did I say? I didn't even say his name."

"You didn't have to. I know you are talking about Blake." I roughly inspected the rest of my cat's body for the sticky goop. I'd gotten most of it off, so I grabbed a towel to dry him off.

"Blake would probably appreciate a phone call or something."

"I'll leave that for Jake to do. He's his partner, after all." I vigorously rubbed his head while Treacle purred madly. His green eyes twinkled. *"You are lucky you are so cute, cat, or I'd have made a coat of you or something. I'll have you stuffed and mounted in the front window."*

I kissed his head when I was finished. He quickly sprang off the bathroom counter and darted out the door. Whatever it was about getting wet that made animals run around the house was always good for a couple of laughs.

Without thinking, I dropped the towels in the hamper and went to Bea and Jake's room. Jake was still next to her, talking to her like she was wide-awake. Peanut Butter was curled up at her feet, purring softly. I stroked the cat as I stood at the end of the bed.

"How is she?"

"I can't tell." Jake smiled sadly.

"How are you?"

"My eyesight is coming back." He smiled. "You are a big pink blur."

"That's right. I am." I took a seat next to him on the bed. Bea looked like a red-headed sleeping beauty.

"She's going to be fine, Jake. She would never let something like a spell keep her from you. You guys have that weird radar love thing going on." I was trying to cheer Jake up, but it wasn't working.

"I don't know what I'm going to do without her, Cath."

"What are you talking about? She's right here, and she's going to be fine." I folded my arms and looked at my cousin. "And see, this really makes me mad. Even after all she's been through with a spooky trying to sink his mitts in her, she still comes out looking ready for a photo shoot." I shook my head. "You're a lucky man, Jake."

"But what if she isn't the same Bea when she wakes up? What if she still...feels the same way about...me?"

"Oh, right." I sighed. "You mean how are you going to handle the several missing days of smooches and I-love-yous that got skipped because of her ailment? That'll be something the two of you need to work out."

"You know what I mean, Cath. What if she still wants a divorce?"

"Of course she doesn't. Look, we can only wait. She's probably not eaten right in the past couple of days, and sleep was not on her list of things to do. Give her a chance to heal herself. Once she does, you guys will be back to your old-fashioned, disgusting selves."

Jake smiled as he took Bea's hand in his and gently stroked it.

"Aunt Astrid said you were covered in some kind of membrane when you came out of that vortex thing. I'd have paid money to see that."

"Oh, Jake. It's all in a day's work." I sniffed, cleared my throat, and adjusted my collar. "There isn't a day that goes by that I'm not covered in slime at least once at some point."

Jake chuckled.

"It was like gray boogers. It was totally gross. But it could have been worse."

"Yeah. You could have been pooped out."

"Thanks, Jake." I stifled my laugh so as not to disturb Bea.

She did look like she was just sleeping. *Just taking a rest,* I thought to myself as I scratched Peanut Butter behind the ears before leaving the room. I puttered around the house and talked with my aunt about things of no real importance. We were all waiting for Jake to call for us to tell us that Bea was awake or that her eyes were open. Something. But each hour that went by only led to another hour and another.

"Is this normal?" I asked my aunt.

"I don't know what's normal in this case," she admitted. "I don't have a reference that tells what happens when a person is pulled from the maw of the abyss."

"Maw of the abyss? Yikes." I looked at Aunt Astrid with my nose wrinkled.

"Well, that's what it was. You should know. You

were in it." She pulled her lips down at the ends and shrugged.

"I feel so helpless. And Jake asked me what he's supposed to do if she wakes up and is no different. What if she still wants a divorce and hates him? Heck, hates all of us?" I furrowed my eyebrows.

"We just won't know until we know." My aunt stroked my hair. "You don't have to wait here. You can go home if you want."

"I might. Just to get the mail and change into my own clothes. Call me if there is any change?" I asked as I walked to the door, scooping up a sleepy Treacle in the process.

"Of course." My aunt waved as she grabbed the tea kettle and took it to the sink to fill up. I expected to hear from my aunt later that day. Then, when the sun started to set, my gut said that would be the time. I'd get a phone call, or maybe even Jake would come by and tell me she was awake. But nothing happened.

"Do you think the Medusa bugaboo still has its hooks in her?" I asked Treacle as we tried to eat a cup of soup and watch an old movie.

"I didn't sense anything. Besides, you blew it to bits. Remember? That would be one tough hombre if it still had

staying power after it was disintegrated into a million pieces."

"*Oh yeah. I tried to put that out of my mind,*" I said, trying to focus on the movie. It certainly wasn't what I needed to keep my mind off Bea. Not to mention that I hadn't heard anything about Tom. "*Tom is in the same boat as Bea. I wonder how he's doing.*"

"*I just love Tom.*" Treacle purred.

"*I know you do,*" I said sadly. Without uttering another word, I quickly slipped on a pair of jeans and a T-shirt. "*I'm going to go out for a while.*"

"*I wouldn't go to the hospital alone if I were you. Remember, Patience is still there.*" Treacle sat up on his haunches.

"*I'm not going to the hospital. I'm going…to see Blake.*"

🦋 23 🦋

GRAY ALIENS

"*R*eally?"

I didn't like Treacle's tone.

"*I'm losing my mind just waiting around,*" I told Treacle. "*I need something to distract me from worrying about Bea and Tom, and this is as good an option as any.*"

"*Are you sure? Television is a good option and doesn't usually get you in any trouble.*"

I scooted off the end of my bed, leaving Treacle right in the middle, where he quickly curled himself up in a tight ball.

"*How can I get in trouble with Blake?*"

It felt good to be behind the wheel of the car. A person could be on autopilot and clear their head a little. I had the window rolled down, and the cool nighttime air was pleasant.

Funny, I wasn't tired, but I didn't really have that much energy. My mind was alert, but I couldn't stay focused. And there was nothing that Blake could do to help me. I just wanted to talk to him. Part of me said I would find an answer there. But I didn't even know what the question was. At least I didn't want to admit what the question was. Not yet.

I showed up at the police station, happy to see Blake's car was still in the parking lot. I knew where he lived, but showing up at his bachelor pad was something I wasn't ready to do. When I walked inside, I saw Steve Furdeck, the guy who seemed to always be manning the front desk.

"Hi, Steve. Is Blake around?"

"What do you need to see him for?" he asked.

"Well, we've been planning on opening a whorehouse in the middle of town. I wanted to see if he got all the paperwork." I put my hands on my hips.

"Jeez, Cath. No need to be so rude."

"No need to be so nosey, Steve."

I lazily paced around the bright lobby. There was a display of badges posted on the wall of officers who retired over the past fifty years. Across from it was another display of several officers who had lost their lives in the line of duty. It included one canine.

I always thought it was a beautiful thing that they recognized what the dogs did and treated them like regular members of the force. If only they knew how much those animals loved their jobs, they'd be even more amazed by them. I heard Roxanne, one of the newer German shepherds, barking her love for her partner while nearly chewing the padded arm off his training suit. It was so touching. But I had to keep it to myself. The Wonder Falls Police Department wasn't ready to know I talked to animals.

"Cath?"

When I turned around and saw Blake, my heart jumped. He looked like he'd had a shower and changed into a different brown suit. The usual loose tie around his neck was missing.

"Hi." I looked at Steve, who was watching both of us.

"Is everything all right?"

"Yeah. Is there somewhere we can talk in private?" I bugged my eyes out at Steve, who quickly looked down at the papers in his hand.

"Sure. Let's go outside."

The stars were out, and there weren't any clouds.

Crickets were chirping, and I could hear the hoot of an owl off in the distance.

"That always has been and always will be a spooky sound," Blake said as we walked toward his car.

"What, the owl?" If only he knew what that wise old bird was saying, he'd blush with embarrassment.

"Yes. You know, some people consider owls harbingers of death. My grandmother used to say if you heard an owl hooting at night, it meant someone was going to die." Blake looked at me. "She was the comedian of my family."

I looked up at him with my nose wrinkled until I realized he was telling a joke. Then I scoffed and smiled.

"Some people also say they indicate where alien sightings take place," he continued. "UFOs are spotted where there are high populations of owls, especially those white ones that resemble the gray aliens."

"Do you believe in aliens?" I asked.

"Let's just say I haven't ruled them out completely." He put his hands on his hips, and I could smell his cologne. Why did he have to smell so good? And the way the light from the station highlighted his square jaw and cheekbones. This was a totally unfair advantage he had, and I wasn't even sure if I was playing the game.

"I don't know why I came out here," I muttered, suddenly feeling terribly foolish. "I know Jake is out. Have you heard anything about Tom? Has his condition changed?"

I hated the fact that my voice held almost no emotion when I asked about Tom. Blake would have to be a total dunce to not have noticed it himself.

"One of the nurses there said she'd call me immediately if there was any news. I haven't heard from her." He still kept studying me.

"Well, no news is good news, they say. I guess I better head back home and see how Bea is feeling." I started to walk to my car. "I'm sorry I bothered you, Blake. I know you've got crime to fight."

"I can't do it on an empty stomach," he said, rubbing his belly.

"You haven't eaten today?"

"Not yet. When you work nights, it is a little harder to stay on a schedule. But on the flip side, there is rarely a rush, and I never have to wait long for my food." He took a step toward me. "Care to join me for lunch at...twelve forty-five at night?"

"I could eat." I smiled.

Yes, part of me thought I should have a scarlet letter stitched across my chest. But another part of me looked down at my bare ring finger. I wasn't married. I wasn't even going steady. I was a grown woman, and I wanted to have something to eat with the handsome and intelligent Detective Blake Samberg. Was that a crime?

"Do you like hamburgers?" he asked as if the answer could possibly be no.

"Of course I do."

"Great. I know just the place." We got into his unmarked sedan and drove to the outskirts of Wonder Falls.

"There sure are a lot of wooded areas and tall grassy places along this route. You think there are any bodies dumped back there?"

"It's always a possibility," Blake replied without skipping a beat. He also went on to tell me a couple of interesting statistics regarding the usual dumping grounds of serial killers. It was fascinating.

"Serial killers are so selfish," I muttered matter-of-factly. "It's bad enough they are doing what they are doing. But they leave their families holding the bags. Like that guy in Wisconsin who was eating people. His dad was a nice man. He was heartbroken when that all came into the light. You'd think that maybe they'd consider how it might affect their parents before they went off the deep end."

"If only it were that simple," Blake said as we walked into a greasy spoon where the waitress waved to Blake and the short order cook called out hello.

"I know. It never is. I'm talking like I know, and I know nothing about it. Heck, I know nothing about pretty much everything." I chuckled as I slid into one of the many open booths.

"That isn't true," Blake said as he slid in across from me. "You have that gift like what's his name. Doctor Dolittle."

I swallowed hard and looked for signs of teasing in his face. There were none.

"What are you talking about?"

Just then the waitress who waved at Blake as we walked in came to our table to take our orders.

"Hey, Detective." She smiled, her eyes practically disappearing in the wrinkles caused by her chubby cheeks. "Your usual?"

"Make it two, Bernice. Bernice, this is Cath Greenstone. Cath, this is Bernice."

I reached up to shake her hand as she got wide-eyed. Her hand was soft except for the rings she wore on just about every finger.

"Greenstone. Do you know the folks who operate that cute little café downtown?" Bernice gushed.

"Yeah. My aunt owns it. I work there too."

"We saw that place in the paper and have been dying to stop in. I just love tea. I am just dying to try the lavender mint tea with the infused honey I read about. It sounds wonderful."

"That is my cousin Bea's specialty." For some reason, the mention of Bea to this sweet waitress made the waterworks burst to life.

"Oh dear. Did I say something wrong?" Bernice's face was shocked and distraught.

"No. I'm sorry. My cousin is sick. That's all." I looked at Blake, who I'd never seen look so worried. "I'm sure she'll be just fine. I'm just worried about her."

"I'm sorry, honey." Bernice was just beside herself.

"It's all right, Bernice," Blake said. "We'll take those burgers to go. Throw in a couple of sodas too."

"You got it, Detective."

Bernice hustled back behind the counter, and I

could see her telling the cook what had happened, shrugging her shoulders and shaking her head. The poor thing had no idea what set me off. Heck, even I wasn't sure except that the overwhelming guilt I was feeling was just becoming too much.

"I'll take you home, Cath," Blake said.

I nodded as I blew my nose in a paper napkin. This was awful. Here Blake was being super nice, and all I could do was fall apart over the mention of Bea. I guess the whole day had taken its toll on me, and I barely realized it.

When Bernice brought us our takeout, I apologized to her. She didn't do a thing wrong. I just said quickly that my cousin was sick and I was worried about her. She was such a good person. I invited her to the café and hoped she'd accept. When we walked out of there, I was sure the woman was probably telling the cook, "I'm not going to that café if they are serving up crazy on a platter like that."

Blake pulled out of the parking lot and drove in the direction of my house.

"Are you going to tell me what happened back there?"

My heart was beating hard, and I decided that this was all or nothing. I was going to spill my guts and let them fall where they may, or something like that. "How much did Jake tell you?" I started.

Blake said he had told Jake he thought Bea was acting strange not long after we started the case with Mrs. Kitt.

I sighed. "Right. Okay. Here goes."

24
MOTLEY CREW

I explained it all, including how Mrs. Kitt's heart exploded, making sure Blake knew it had nothing to do with the one-in-a-trillion statistic he mentioned. I told him about Bea getting caught in the mirror and the Medusa Praesentia spell that was causing her to act so out of character.

"I knew something was wrong with her when she came to the station," Blake said. My stomach sank.

"What did she do there?" I asked carefully.

"Let's just say it was obvious she wasn't herself. She made me a couple of offers that had I been a dishonest man, I might have taken her up on. But after I talked to her briefly, she left and said she was going back home."

I wanted to know what she said, and yet I didn't.

She'd made enough clear when she was shouting at me and Jake and Aunt Astrid.

"Did you tell Jake what she said?"

"No. I don't think I ever will," Blake replied without looking at me.

"You have to understand she wasn't herself. And she's still not better." I felt tears coming to my eyes again. "Blake, she's like those people that get certain kinds of brain tumors. They press on a part of their brain, and what was a normally nice, sweet person transforms into a foulmouthed stranger. They don't even know they are doing it. You wouldn't blame a person who had cancer. Please don't blame her."

He took my hand in his. It was warm and strong.

"Blake, my family isn't like other families. We're witches. But not like the movies or old-time books say we are. Don't get me wrong, there are some bad ones out there putting curses on people and stuff, but that isn't us. Nope. Every time I wanted to put a curse on someone, my aunt stopped me. So, no accusations of revenge would ever stand up in a witch trial. Not where the Greenstones are concerned."

"I know," he replied.

"What? You know? How?"

"Jake told me."

My jaw hit the floor of the car.

"When?"

Blake took a deep breath and stretched his fingers out from the steering wheel. He was quiet for a moment, but before I could repeat myself, he opened his mouth to speak.

"I think you and Tom had just started dating." He swallowed.

"You've known all that time and acted like you knew nothing?" I looked out the window and huffed before turning and punching him in the arm.

"Hey, that's assaulting a police officer!" he griped, rubbing his arm with his other hand.

"Great! Take me in, and tell all the guys how I beat you up. That'll get you the street cred you deserve," I grumbled. "How come you didn't say anything?"

"I didn't really believe Jake."

"But you guys are partners. Why would he lie to you?"

"I don't know if you've noticed, but Jake acts different around Bea all the time. He's not the same guy, and I'm not saying it in a bad or derogatory way. When he said she could manipulate someone's heart and feelings, I thought he was just being dramatic."

"She's an empath. And she's in trouble. And there isn't anything I can do about it."

"And you can talk to the animals?"

"Mostly just cats. I can communicate with most, but cats are the real talkers." I shrugged. "It's not as glamorous as Bea or Aunt Astrid's gifts."

"Your aunt can see different dimension and the future."

"That's right. Did Jake tell you that too?" I shook my head and reached inside the bag, grabbing a few fingers' worth of French fries and shoveling them into my mouth.

"Nope. She did."

"What? Why would she tell you that?"

"She said she saw something in the future that would require I know the truth." He shrugged.

"Did she say what it was?"

Blake shook his head no.

I took a deep breath and another handful of fries.

"Hey, some of those are mine, you know. I'm on duty. I need my strength," he said and didn't sound like he was playing at all.

"Too bad," I said with a mouthful. "Just wait until I see that motley crew of a family. I'm going to have quite a few things to say to them. Here I've been tiptoeing around telling you my big secret, and you already knew. The big secret was don't tell Cath that everyone in Wonder Falls knows she's a witch."

"I don't know what you're getting upset over," Blake interrupted. "I didn't think you were ever going to tell me."

"Don't turn this around like I did something wrong. I kept my mouth shut for once. Do you know what a monumental achievement that is? Only to find out my whole family blabbed it all over the place."

When we pulled down my street, Aunt Astrid was walking toward my house. She was in her pajamas and a shawl. Blake pulled the car over, and she came hurrying to us.

"She's awake," Aunt Astrid panted.

That was all I needed to hear. I opened the passenger door and was about to hop out but grabbed the food, stuck my tongue out at Blake, and hurried to Bea's house.

I knew Aunt Astrid would invite Blake in. But I couldn't wait for him to park the car. As soon as I pushed open the door, I heard the most wonderful sound. It was Bea and Jake. They were laughing.

I bounded up the stairs and knocked on the door.

"You guys were alone for a few minutes. Do you need to put your clothes back on?"

"Cath?"

I swallowed hard as I peeked in, smiling. Bea was

sitting up. The normal rosiness was back in her cheeks. Jake kissed Bea on the top of her head as he got up from the bed.

"Burgers?" he asked as he approached.

"They're both mine," I grumbled as he took the bag from me and gave me a peck on top of the head, too, before heading downstairs.

"How are you feeling?" I crept in slowly.

"Well." She started to cry. "Not so good, Cath."

I hurried to her side and sat down, taking her hands in mine. "Why? What hurts?"

She tapped her chest. "I remember." She cried. "I remember it all. It was like I was outside myself watching and listening to a movie. I was helpless to stop it. To stop myself from dressing that way and acting that way and saying the things I said. Cath, I'm sorry. You are my best friend. I love you so much, and I'm sorry for the things I said. I didn't mean them. Not at all."

"Bea, I know that." I looked at her curiously. "Do you really think I'd hold it against you? You were in trouble. And now you're safe. And no Medusa Prae-sentia is going to keep me from you. We're a team. Whether you like it or not."

"Cath." She hugged me tightly. "How did I get so lucky to have you in my life?"

"Right back at you, cuz."

When she leaned back, I had to wipe my eyes with the hem of my shirt.

"But there is one thing I'm not sorry I said." She cleared her throat and leaned back slightly as if she were afraid a slap might be coming her way. "I told you Blake loves you. He does. And you love him. Lord, I made a fool of him and myself. I'll have to mend that fence sooner rather than later."

"So, you think that just because you were in a pickle with the Medusa Praesentia, I'm going to go easy on you? You're wrong, sista." I sniffled. "Blake squealed on all of you too. Jake, Aunt Astrid, you... well, wait. He didn't mention you in particular, but you'll just suffer guilt by association."

"What are you talking about?"

I took a deep breath and smiled. "It can wait until you're feeling better."

Jake came back into the room with a glass of seltzer water with sliced lime in it and a straw. He kissed Bea on the head, the cheek, quickly on the lips.

"Gross. I'm out of here. We'll talk when you aren't being pawed by Jake."

"Don't go far, Cath. We have something that needs to be done," Bea said.

"I live across the street, remember?" I winked. "Jake, take care of her."

"You know I will, Cath."

I went back downstairs and saw Aunt Astrid sitting with Blake. I arched my right eyebrow as I approached them. "What are you two talking about?"

"Nothing," Aunt Astrid said, and it was obvious the way she was trying not to laugh that she was lying. I picked up the white carryout sack that had delicious grease spots forming on it.

"I'm going home now that Bea is up and back to her normal self. And I'm taking my food."

"Half of that is my food," Blake said.

"Then you better just come with me because I'm eating it at my house with my cat in front of my television." I kissed my aunt quickly on the cheek. "I'll talk to you later."

Blake kissed Aunt Astrid, too, and swiped the bag from my hand as he opened the door for me. I hated that I was loving his attention. Tom was still laid up without anyone being able to help him, and I was falling for someone else at the same time.

You aren't falling for him. You fell for Blake the minute you laid eyes on him.

That pesky conscience never knew when to shut up.

Blake and I did enjoy the burgers at my house. We talked about some of the cases he was working on, and I didn't bring back up the fact that I came from a long line of witches. Why should I? Everyone else had already filled in the gaps.

He left at about two in the morning, promising that he'd talk to me later in the day. I didn't think there was anything odd about that until Bea called me at around eight in the morning.

"Are you ready?"

"Ready for what?" I asked, wiping the sleep from my eyes.

"Ready to go help Tom?"

25

BLACK PLAGUE

"I feel like I'm going to war," I said as Bea drove to the hospital. "Driving really slowly, with wind-chimey music to get me pumped and ready for battle."

"Aren't you funny? The speed limit is thirty-five on this street." Bea sounded just like her old self.

"Yes, that means you can go forty, maybe even forty-two," I urged.

"All right, girls," Aunt Astrid interrupted. "We are going to need a special protection spell that will not only protect us from what we know can be lurking in a hospital but from what we don't know. This is going to be tricky."

She opened her big spell book to a page she had dog-eared.

"Can we do this in the car?" I muttered. "Maybe we should pull over. Or if you need more room, you can use the back seat. I can get out and walk and still keep up with Bea."

"Ha ha." Bea rolled her eyes in the rearview mirror. There was a glow around her that made me feel happy. It was so good to see her back to herself.

"No. We'll do this in the garage of the hospital once we park. I'll get a better lay of the land that way," my aunt said.

"Jake and Blake are already on their way?" I asked.

"Yes. They promised to run interference until Bea can assess Tom's condition," Aunt Astrid said.

"Are you sure you are up to it?" I asked.

"I'm dying to do it." She shook her head. "That woman was definitely up to something when we came here the first time. I was just too out of it to help. I just hope that Tom's condition hasn't gotten worse."

We pulled into the underground visitor parking garage, and Bea led us around to an isolated corner for us to get ready.

With a wave of her hand, Aunt Astrid turned the security camera in the opposite direction. Bea took my hand, and I felt her reading my aura before she patted me on the back. She did the same to her mother.

"All our vitals are looking good," she whispered.

Aunt Astrid gave us each a white candle to represent our familiars who couldn't come with. She lit them all in addition to a bundle of sage that also had fresh coriander wrapped with the dry leaves.

I knew coriander had some strong medicinal properties. When my aunt reached into her purse that was really a huge sack embroidered with multi-colored ribbons in a striped pattern and fringe hanging off the bottom, she pulled out a clove of garlic, a ginger root, and a plastic baggie of cayenne pepper.

"This is an old spell. It was prevalent during the Black Plague. I'm thinking that it might be just what we need to keep whatever Patience is conjuring up away from us long enough for us to help Tom." She smirked. "I'll save the worst part for last."

"Worst part?" I looked at Bea, who shrugged. "What worst part?"

Aunt Astrid shushed me, so I pinched my lips together and looked at Bea.

"*Placidus autem non imbellis,*" she muttered as she waved the sage-coriander mixture over us. Then, with the garlic clove in one hand and the ginger in the other, we were marked on our heads, our throats, our chests, and our hands.

"And now, for the hard part." She took the baggie of cayenne pepper and pulled out a small, hand-carved wooden spoon. "Open wide."

"Ugh. We have to swallow that?"

She nodded. "I'll go first." Down the hatch my aunt swallowed the teaspoonful. "There will be side effects, so let's hurry."

I held my nose, took a deep breath, and opened wide while squeezing my eyes shut. In one gulp, I swallowed the powder. It was like it just ran to my eyes, making them burn and run.

"Uh! It's worse than I imagined." I desperately wished for a Coke. "Why didn't you warn us? We could have had some Mountain Dew in the car, or water even."

"It doesn't work if you water it down," my aunt muttered as Bea took her medicine without incident.

I stared at her. "Nothing?"

"That's tasty." She licked her lips. "I didn't mind that at all. It really opened my sinuses."

"Aunt Astrid, I think I'm going to be sick." I clutched my stomach.

"That's the whole idea, honey." She handed me a plastic bag, and I dashed off behind the car to wretch. I wasn't there long before I was feeling much better. Really good, as a matter of fact. Aunt Astrid had the same response as I did. When she appeared from around the corner, she was feeling better too.

"You're just as pleasant as punch, aren't you?" I asked Bea.

"Didn't bother me in the least." She raised her chin proudly.

"Well, now I know what to make for you for your special birthday dinner," I replied.

"You are a riot. A regular comedian."

"I am, aren't I?"

"All right, girls. You've been cleansed from the inside out. We've got nothing for Patience to latch onto. Be brave. Be calm. And most of all, be careful. Let's go."

We took the elevator to the lobby and were told by a kind older volunteer named Velma that Tom Warner was in intensive care.

"It says here that only immediate family is allowed to visit. Are you family?" she asked innocently. I didn't want to get Velma in trouble. But this was a matter of life or death. I looked to Aunt Astrid, but it was Bea who stepped up.

"I'm his sister." She touched Velma's hand. "This is my mother-in-law and sister-in-law. It's been hard on us. Especially since I haven't spoken to him or my mother in a long time. Isn't it a shame it takes a tragedy to bring people together?"

"Better late than never, my mother always said." Velma smiled and gave us each a visitor's pass with today's date, the floor, and room number on it. We left for the elevators.

"Do you think Jake and Blake had any luck getting her away from Tom's bedside?" I asked nervously. The last thing I wanted was another confrontation.

"We'll see," Aunt Astrid replied.

"Well, that's reassuring," I muttered. "Don't throw me a bone just to make me feel better. Patience didn't call you a whore."

My aunt patted me on the shoulder as we piled in and went to the third floor. Aunt Astrid stepped off first. Her steps were sure but careful. She was moving around things only she could see, nodding to entities only visible to her eyes. I scanned the room for the devil. Patience Warner. So far, I hadn't seen her anywhere.

Jake and Blake were waiting outside Tom's door as we approached.

"Where is she?" I asked.

"She wasn't here when we got here," Blake said. "How are you holding up?"

"I'm good. My aunt tried to poison me with a spoonful of cayenne pepper." I smirked.

"That's what that smell is." He nodded and reached into his pocket to offer me a mint, but Aunt Astrid shook her head.

"Sorry. Gotta stay funky for this." I shrugged and walked past him to look in the window to Tom's room. I could see his feet underneath the blanket, but the curtain around his bed was pulled out so I couldn't see his face.

"Look, whatever happens in there, don't worry about Patience Warner," Blake said. "I promise she won't get to you like before."

"Thanks," I said, looking up at him. I turned to my aunt and bounced my eyebrows. "Should I get the ball rolling?"

"You go in first, Cath. Recite the words we practiced. Then I'll follow, and finally Bea will join us at our full strength to finish the job. The boys will keep anyone from coming in. Right, guys?"

"That's right, Mom." Jake kissed Bea on the cheek again. "Good luck."

I took a deep breath and walked into the room.

26

HIDING

I had to shake my head because there were no flowers or cards from the precinct. As I quietly walked into the room, letting the door shut behind me, I thought that even if I wasn't going to continue seeing Tom, I was going to send a real complaint to his precinct. What kind of men didn't support their own when they got hurt in the line of duty?

But as I rounded the curtain and peeked at the side table, I saw the garbage can filled with flowers and cards.

Tom's face was pale and sad. I stooped down and saw the cards were from his fellow officers.

"Who threw these away?" I muttered.

"What are you doing here?"

I looked at Tom, expecting to see his eyes open, but he was out of it, with a tube down his throat. Where did that voice come from?

Standing next to me, hiding inside the folded-up end of the sliding curtain was Patience. I jumped back but not quick enough. She hit me with the book she was holding. It was old, and I saw a crude pentagram on the cover.

"Patience." I covered my mouth where she'd knocked me. "Where did you get that book?"

"I said you weren't welcome here," she hissed.

"That book, Patience. Where did you get it?" It didn't take a scholar of the occult to know that what she was using for a little light reading was not good for her.

"You filled his mind with poison. Now you are back to finish the job. Well, you and your little coven are not going to get away with it. I'll stop you."

"That's not true, Patience, and you know it." I scowled. "I'm here to help him, but you want to keep him sick and hurt just to keep him away from me. You know what I call that? I call that loco." I made circles around my temple. "You're going to need a bigger army than you and that book to keep me from helping Tom."

Patience chuckled. She opened her book and

started to mutter off a bunch of creepy-sounding words while she licked her lips and giggled.

From the shadows, I could see figures. They were large and black and looming. At first, I thought my eyes were playing tricks on me. But then I saw one of them step out of the wall. He was wearing a hat and a black jacket, and he had no face.

"Oh, really? You're using the men in black just for you?" I spat. "How much more selfish can you get? These guys are supposed to help some people along their way, not stand around and play manservant to the likes of you."

"They are here to stop you. They will be helping you along your way, Cath Greenstone. They'll be helping you along your way to hell."

"Silence, imposter!" Aunt Astrid shouted. She pointed her finger at Patience, who shrank behind her book. "You dare use the occupants of the nether-world as if they are yours." Her hand went up, and Patience clutched her own throat. "What have you done?"

Patience's head began to wobble back and forth and side to side. She clawed at her throat as she continued to fight Aunt Astrid until, finally, in a raspy voice, she confessed.

"He will remain in this sleep until my debt is paid," she said.

"What is your debt, and who is it to?" Aunt Astrid asked, giving the old broad another good shake.

"I wanted her away from him." She jerked her chin at me. "I wanted him to leave her. You are dirty and filthy and…"

"Yeah, yeah, Patience, I know," I said. "Get to the point."

She didn't like that I wasn't interested in her monologue. Her eyes narrowed, and had Aunt Astrid not been there, she would have scratched my eyes out. But as it was, we were two against, well, Patience and her handful of MIB.

"I promised a child. Any child would do. Any age would do. And I was willing to pay the price once I knew you were gone. The serpent wanted any child."

"Well thank goodness I came back," I replied. "How could you? Do you know how many women in this country don't like their in-laws? Still, they don't go promising babies to demons. That's it. Put that book down. You and I are gonna have a go."

I was ready to tear her limb from limb when my aunt raised her hands.

"I am afraid you'll have to answer to the serpent

because you are not going to fulfill your end of the bargain."

"No!" Patience screamed and was just about to charge Aunt Astrid when she was lifted into the air. Her legs kicked, and she flailed her arms. Her round glasses fell to the floor, cracking.

I stepped up to Tom and recited my words, just as Aunt Astrid told me to when we prepared for this. Though, now that I was standing there, watching a woman who willingly made a deal with a devil, I didn't know if I really was prepared. Didn't she realize that Tom was her baby? What would she have done if he were taken as a child? I shuddered to think about it.

"With one hand, I bind you, Patience Warner. With the other, I steal your voice. You will never call on the serpent again. He will be denied his prize. You will not give it a baby." Patience fell to the ground. She looked up at me and screamed a horrifying silent scream. Her face contorted in pain and anger.

"A baby?" Bea asked as she slowly walked in.

I shook my head as Bea walked up to the bed. She stepped over Patience, who scooted back to the corner where she had been when I first arrived. With mad determination, she began flipping through the book for some way to get back at us. To stop us. But it was too late.

Bea put her hand on Tom's head. Her face contorted in sadness.

"It's all right, Tom. It's all right," she said. "Stay with me. Just stay right where you are."

Aunt Astrid could see the kaleidoscope of colors that were being pulled from Tom's body. She saw the sparks and the flames and the shafts of light that Bea controlled and moved and twisted. Things were torn away while others were mended.

All I could see was Bea flailing her hands over Tom. Her eyes were closed, and her forehead was starting to get shiny with sweat.

"You stay back," Bea said with clenched teeth. I looked at Patience, but she'd collapsed into the chair and was twitching and rolling her eyes. "I don't answer to you. You stay back."

Bea was getting tough with someone. I remembered the candles and pulled them out of my aunt's purse. I lit them all and placed them at the head, the foot, and in the middle of Tom's bed. The cats would help remotely. If I listened hard, I could hear each one of them fighting off the spirits. Peanut Butter made me smile, as he had gotten so much tougher over the past couple of days. Marshmallow was loud and foreboding. And Treacle was the strong, silent type.

"I said you stay back!" Bea shouted. "Don't even think about it!" Her hands moved so fast they were like a blur. She was breathing heavily, as if she were trying to run uphill. "I'm almost there, Tom. Don't give up! Stay with me!"

The cats fought. Aunt Astrid held Patience at bay, and I stood there waiting.

Finally, Bea's eyes popped open. She gasped for breath, as if she'd been underwater the whole time. She whirled around to Patience, grabbed her by the collar, and through clenched teeth, said, "I ought to feed you to that snake."

27

BIGFOOT

I'm not ashamed to say I stood there in shock and awe. Bea had never, never spoken to anyone that way. Even when she was under the spell of the Medusa Praesentia, you could tell it wasn't really her. This was totally her.

She dropped Patience back in the chair where the woman slumped. Aunt Astrid released the MIB to go about their ghoulish business of tapping people for the hereafter.

I took Tom's hand and squeezed it. "Hey, are you in there?" He squeezed my hand back instantly. His eyes blinked and opened, and when he looked at me, he started to cry.

"Don't do that," I said, wiping a tear from my

own eye. "You'll choke on your own snot. Let me get a nurse."

"You stay with him." Bea smiled.

"Unbelievable. My cousin can do what she did and still look like she's ready for her close-up. Crazy." I looked down at Tom. I was sure that when this moment came, I'd be a ball of nerves, hemming and hawing and tripping over my tongue because I couldn't say *I love you* to him. As I looked at him, helpless as he was, I got the feeling he knew. I also got the feeling he wasn't mad.

Aunt Astrid put her body between Tom and his mother. The woman still couldn't talk, and it was as if her body had decided it had had enough. She sat in the chair like a rag doll.

When the nurses appeared, they cleared us all out. Aunt Astrid took Patience and asked Jake to give them both a lift to her house. They verified her address from her wallet in her purse. Patience went without putting up a fuss.

There was something very wrong there, but I walked up to Blake and told him what had happened.

"Were you really going to fight her?" he asked seriously.

"They tell you to talk smack in self-defense classes." I tugged at my jeans and rocked on my heels. "It throws off the attacker if you start acting like you really want them to try it."

"Well, I'd be scared of you," Blake said, not cracking a smile.

"You of all people better be," I added.

We waited around for a while. Once Patience was at her home, Aunt Astrid put a spell on her and the house that would keep her there and safe until there was something that could be done with her. Bea stayed with me to wait until the doctors told us we could visit Tom. Blake brought us lunch and then left to get back to the station.

"It was nice of him to bring us food," Bea said as she devoured a spinach salad, a slice of garlic bread, and a slice of chocolate cake for dessert.

"You know he brought you a cake with sugar and flour." I pointed at her empty tray with a French fry.

"I'm starving. Beggars can't be choosers." She wiped her mouth on the paper napkin.

"If either of you would like to go in, he can have a visitor," the nurse said as she came out of his room. "We just ask that you go one at a time. Even after all that sleep, he still needs to rest."

"Go on, Cath. Take your time," Bea said as she took the remaining bits of my lunch off my lap.

I wiped my mouth on the back of my hand,

straightened my jeans, and headed in. Tom was sitting up. He smiled that handsome smile at me as soon as he saw me.

"This is ridiculous," I said. "The lengths you'll go to get someone to bring you breakfast in bed."

"Don't make me laugh." He winced and held his side. "I got shot, you know."

"Yeah. I know." I carefully scooted up on the bed and took hold of his hand. "So, how are you feeling now?"

"I'm okay. Considering." He looked at me so kindly. It was like he'd read my mind and was prepared for what I had to say. Except, I didn't know what I wanted to say. "I'm sorry you had to see all that...with my mother."

"You were aware of it?" Now it was my turn to wince.

"Cath, you have to believe me when I tell you that she wasn't always like this. Something has happened to her. I don't know if it can be explained through a doctor's exam or if it's something more...spiritual."

"You don't need to explain anything to me, Tom," I said. "You needed help. That was all I saw. I couldn't just sit by."

"You saved my life."

"Actually, Bea did. I just brought backup." I winked.

"You know I saw them all. Treacle, Marshmallow. That little guy has really grown. How long have I been out of it?"

"Just a little over a week or so. Maybe two weeks at the most." I smoothed his hair. "You probably need a shower."

"I'll request a sponge bath and get one of those younger nurses to give it to me." He smirked.

"Well, you know I won't stop you there." I chuckled.

"I know."

The way he said those words made me get choked up inside. My chest tightened, squeezing tears out of my eyes and holding my breath tightly inside of me. I patted his hand.

"We had a lot of fun, though, right?" I said, sniffling.

"I've never met a woman like you before, Cath." He smiled.

"And you never will again. I'm like the elusive Bigfoot. Once you see it for yourself, you'll never be the same." Tom laughed and then winced, and that made me laugh and shake the bed. It was a vicious circle of laughter and wincing.

"So, what are you going to do once you get out of here?"

"I'm going to take Mom to get checked out. I'll be on desk duty for a long while. I don't know. I'm thinking maybe I need a change of scenery."

"Where would you go?"

"My sister lives in Kansas. Her husband is a doctor. I think that sounds like the best bet. I'm sure I could get a transfer arranged from the department," he said, looking off toward the window that was shut. "It would be hard to say goodbye to everything and everyone I've gotten to know here."

"Yeah. But you're a likeable guy...most of the time. I'm sure you'll have friends in no time. And I'm sure you won't have any problems meeting the ladies."

An uncomfortable silence settled over us. I went to move my hand, but Tom wouldn't let go. He brought it to his lips and kissed it. It was a nice gesture, but the tingles weren't there.

"You are one in a million. But you've ruined me for witches."

"That makes more sense than you know." I smirked.

"Cath, I told you I had a couple of psychic experiences, some premonitions that came true." He patted my hand as he talked. "I never thought much of it all until we met. Then I thought that maybe it was something more. Maybe it meant you and I were meant to be together. It was something we had in common. But after what my mother did, I just don't want it."

"I understand." I tilted my head. "It's a gift, but that doesn't make it any less scary or overwhelming."

"I could see her, Cath. I wasn't in a coma like the doctors said. I mean, for all appearances, I was in a coma. But I knew when people were in the room. I knew when my mother was here. I knew when you were here. She wanted me to stay here, and I don't know why." His voice wavered. "I need to go some-place to start over again. There are just too many things here that I feel might trigger her."

"Like me? I've been known to rub people the wrong way." I wiped one of his curls off his forehead.

"Please don't think it means I don't still love you. I do. More than you'll know." I felt my cheeks burn up with embarrassment. "But it would take more than this to keep us together, don't you think?"

"Yeah." I looked down. "Your mom, she's just lost, Tom. She doesn't know what she's doing."

"That's the really tragic part, Cath. She does

know. She's known for some time what she's been doing, and none of it seemed to bother her." It was Tom's turn to look at his hands. He was embarrassed. "But she's my mother. I can't hate her. I can only try to help her."

"Do you know where she got that book from?" I asked, rubbing my chin where she got me good with it.

"What book?"

"Well, it was an old-looking book with a pentagram on the cover." I said it as if the words hurt my mouth to speak them. To be truthful, they did. Tom was the last person in the world I thought should be going through this. He was so good inside.

"I don't know anything about it," he said. "Are you sure it was a pentagram?"

I nodded sadly.

"She's like an alcoholic. She just doesn't know when to quit." He wiped a tear from his eye.

"I think your plan for her is the best idea." I tried to be cheerful, but I had no clue if taking Patience to Kansas would help or a psych evaluation or even one of those deprogrammers they used for people mixed up with cults. This was not my decision to make, and I was glad of it.

"It's all I've got right now."

We sat for a little while longer and chatted. I tried to be as encouraging and optimistic as possible. Had Tom asked, I would have come to visit him again, and I would have even helped him get settled at home while he finished recuperating. But he didn't ask me to. And I didn't offer.

I gave him a hug and a kiss goodbye, and that was it. When I walked out of his room, the person waiting for me was not who I had expected it to be.

28

ALL SMILES

"What are you doing here?" I asked Blake quietly.

"I was waiting for you." He looked at the closed door. "How's he doing?"

"I think Tom is going to be fine. His mother, on the other hand, needs some help. But he might be able to get it for her." I didn't want to tell Blake all the gory details. It wasn't his business. I would have felt like a real gossip had I shared the fact that Patience Warner was, for all intents and purposes, a certifiable devil worshipper. "Hey, I left a burger here with Bea. Now both of them are gone."

"Bea ate it. Then she said she had to get home, so I told her I'd wait for you."

"That can't be. Bea is a vegetarian. You've seen all

the stuff she cooks at her house. Kale and sweet potatoes and tofu." I shivered. "She's just weird that way."

"Well, as sure as I'm sitting here, she polished off that burger in like three bites." Blake shrugged.

"I'll bet it's just some kind of side effect from her ordeal." I nodded. "She'll get over it."

"So, are you going to stick around for a while?" Blake asked as we walked down the corridor of the intensive care unit toward the exit.

"No. I'm going home, and I hope not to come to this hospital again for a long time." I folded my arms over my chest. "It's full of sick people here," I whispered.

Blake nodded as if he concurred with my assessment of the number of ill patients. I rolled my eyes.

"That was a joke?" He looked at me.

"Yeah, Mr. Spock. That was a joke," I replied.

"It was pretty good." He nodded without smiling. "Would you like a lift home?"

"Is that a joke?"

"No. I'm serious." Blake looked at me as if I had annoyed him.

"Yes. I'd like a lift home." I smirked.

"Would you like me to get you another burger?"

"Yeah, since Bea ate mine. I think that's the least

you could do." We bickered back and forth about lunch, about what way to drive home, where he parked, and finally, I had had enough of his statistical reports about abductions and assaults in parking garages.

"Blake, you really are a cornucopia of useless information," I said.

"I've always had this nervous tick that I'd go into great detail about a subject when I was having trouble coping in a situation," he said as we reached his car.

"Are you that nervous in the parking garage? I'm sorry. I didn't know. Look, I won't say anything to anyone, and I promise I'll protect you. I took self-defense classes, remember?"

Blake looked at me like I was shedding my outer skin.

Before I could ask him what the matter was now, he walked right up to me, took me in his arms, and kissed me square on the lips.

At first, I just froze there, stiff as a board in his arms. But the heat from that kiss went from my head to my toes, and before I knew it, I was kissing him back.

"I've been waiting a long time to do that," he said, still holding me.

"You have?"

"Yes." He kissed me again.

"Even with all my background and family history?" I kissed him too.

"Cath, I love your family. Aunt Astrid, Bea, and Jake. The cats. I love it all." He kissed me again and again. "But mostly, I love you."

"You do?" I started to cry. I didn't know why. Okay, yes, I did. Because those were the words I was waiting to hear, and Blake was the man I was waiting to hear them from. "Are you sure?"

"I've never been surer of anything in my life." He looked at me so seriously. His handsome, chiseled face had a touch of stubble that made him look wild. His eyes looked so deeply into mine that I felt safe standing there in the underground garage even after hearing all of his scary statistics.

It was my turn to stand on my tiptoes and kiss Blake on the lips. I didn't know how long we did this, but we finally decided to go home and let everyone in on this new development.

But when we got there, there was something new already brewing.

"Hey. What's going on?" I asked as Blake and I walked into Aunt Astrid's house. Jake and Bea were sitting so close to each other on the couch they could have swapped shirts without anyone knowing. Aunt Astrid was a bundle of excitement as she bustled behind the counter, mixing something that smelled sweet and yummy.

"Hey, guys." Jake was all smiles. He stood up and shook Blake's hand, clapping him on the back.

Bea looked like the cat that had swallowed the canary. I took Jake's spot next to her and yelled to my aunt about what smelled so good.

"Ask Bea," she said mysteriously before going back to her cooking.

"Oh yeah. Thanks for eating my burger. What's up with that? Whatever it is she's cooking in there, I get your piece," I said, playfully nudging my cousin.

"Sorry. Can't share. Need it for the baby."

I looked at Bea and then at Jake. "A baby? You mean like you two nerds are going to have a baby?"

Aunt Astrid squealed with laughter as she clapped her hands in the kitchen.

"I'm going to be an aunt?" I started to cry. Then I gasped. "That's why you said what you did to Patience! I get it now. Oh my gosh, why did you go in there in your condition? Bea, that could have been dangerous." I hugged her tightly.

"He's got his daddy's bravery. I can feel it. And I think he's got just enough of his aunt Cath's stubbornness that he won't give up very often." She smiled and held my hand.

"You know it's a boy already?" I asked.

"I do. And I know that you and Blake have finally made it official." She looked at Blake and winked, to which he nodded back without smiling, looking as handsome as ever.

"How did you know?" I asked.

"I think this little guy will have some psychic abilities that he's already sharing with his mama."

I tried not to cry. "Bea, this is going to be our best adventure yet."

ABOUT THE AUTHOR

Harper Lin is a *USA TODAY* bestselling cozy mystery author.

When she's not reading or writing mysteries, she loves going to yoga classes, hiking, and hanging out with her family and friends.

www.HarperLin.com

Made in the USA
Middletown, DE
12 May 2020

94284894R00158